The CHALET *Next Door*

BY

CASSANDRA JOELLE

Dedicated to my skijoring champion husband, Chad, who helped guide this story towards the finish line.

SKI TRAIL MAP

CHAPTER 1: PRESLEY
ALL ROADS LEAD TO SAGE MOUNTAIN

"A big storm is expected tonight to hit Sage Mountain Ski Area—forecasters are saying up to eighteen inches of powder, just in time for the Winter Games!" The radio alerting me of the upcoming forecast was good news, as I was not trekking these snow-covered roads for poor skiing conditions.

"Did you hear that, Priscilla? Mommy's going to ski powder!" My Shih Tzu didn't seem to care about the upcoming fresh snow. She was all curled up on the passenger seat in her cozy donut bed, atop a heating pad and wearing her cute, lime green sweater. I switched the radio station back to the Christian music channel. As I drove around a bend, majestic mountains came into view.

"Girl's trip, Priscilla! Isn't this fun?" She didn't even look up at me this time, perfectly nestled in her warm seat. "Just me, Jesus, and my Shih Tzu," I laughed, clasping the silver cross necklace I wore. "No man can say I'm too much when it's just me and my doggy." I sighed, remembering just yesterday when I booked this last-minute trip to recharge my internal batteries, but I'd often felt silly about going somewhere alone. I didn't need a man to be happy or complete—I just needed my relationship with God. And besides, Priscilla made the perfect travel companion. I shot another glance at her and now her back was to me.

The song playing was a familiar ballad I had heard in church, as I tried to sing along, but missed all of the beats and lyrics. Priscilla was looking at me again, no doubt judging my terrible voice. I turned it up a notch to drown out my singing right as it ended. "Next up we have a rendition of Hallelujah from one of our local singers right here in Sage Mountain, Wyoming. But before we play it, we have a word from our sponsors about the Winter Games!"

In the last thirty minutes, I'd heard more about the Winter Games than I had about the snowstorm that was supposedly going to hit us. "You do not want to miss Sage Mountain's Winter Games! Hosted by Sage Mountain's Olympic gold medalist ski jumper, Theo McCain. The annual Skijoring Competition at this year's event will have reigning champion,

Ford—" The radio cut out as I drove through a dead spot. I turned it off, seeing as I was only fifteen minutes away from the resort, according to my built-in GPS in my Yukon.

As I drove the winding roads in silence, my mind immediately went back to the anxieties at work. Since becoming a book publisher in Denver, I'd had several highly sought after novels published under my imprint. With waking up every day to a freshly full inbox of new submissions, my life consisted of reading. I read while I brushed my teeth. While I cooked dinner. I no longer had time to watch television or listen to music, as my phone could read the submissions to me while driving.

I reached a breaking point yesterday around 9 in the morning, when my cup of coffee spilled on my blouse, as I was already late for work in epic proportions from oversleeping. I stayed up too late the night before reading manuscript submissions. Once the coffee touched my white silk blouse, I discovered I was burned out. While I was incredibly thankful for the success to which God had made possible at my young age of twenty-six, I had almost no time to myself. I'd begun to lose my identity and forget the things I enjoyed. I lived in Denver, Colorado—just a few hours from some of the greatest skiing in the Rockies—and I couldn't remember the last time I skied. Or, had my phone off. Not checking my email for an hour felt like a rebellion—until now.

Yesterday, I may have had a bit of a meltdown. Some might have considered it a nervous breakdown, but thankfully, Priscilla was my only witness. And now, I was driving to a luxury chalet at the base of a hopping ski resort, Sage Mountain, Wyoming. I'd be merely steps to the brand-new Gondola installed last year, having almost an entire week of relaxation and time away from my team, who were more than capable of handling things. I just needed to give them the opportunity to do so. Right?

According to my therapist, my long singledom had created even more of a powerhouse woman out of me. While men I had met in the last few years had generally thought of me as "too busy" or "too successful," "too this" or "too that," I'd overcompensated in my career. It was a classic chicken and the egg scenario. Was I always this driven to take over the world of publishing, or did men rejecting me make me this way?

I graduated college on a fast track—finishing my degree in three years instead of four. When I signed on at a publishing firm, only a year had passed before they let me have my own imprint, where I was publishing Christian books and novels written by and for readers in my same age group. At times, er—most of the time—it was a lot of pressure to keep up, but I was doing everything I could to stay above water. However, with the agony of my dating experiences, things had felt more strained. Until recently.

The Lord had freed me of those past hurts. I didn't want to hand over the reins and let people take things off my plate. That's why, yesterday, after arriving at work on Monday morning in my still-stained blouse, I promoted my assistant, Jenny, to stand in for me while I was away. Once she got over her deer-in-headlights expression, I thought she accepted the task. I wasn't really sure. I was already out the door.

Truthfully, I was a little nervous how things would be without me there for an entire week. We had a pretty big launch planned for a new devotional book geared towards single women. I admitted I had a bias for the material matter, but I took a deep breath, and I trusted that Jenny could handle things, as she had been by my side for three years. We'd practically built it together.

As I approached the resort, the snow piled high on surrounding roof tops and pine trees was a feast for my eyes. It was as if everything has been sprinkled in sparkling powdered sugar. Smoke was curling from chimneys, and a chill came over me from excitement. "The vacation rental listing mentioned it was close to main street," I said aloud, not that Priscilla cared. As I traversed the main drag, I was charmed by the twinkling lights adorning every tree, light pole, and building and the beautiful ice-skating rink in the center of town. I imagined going there for an evening and sliding around on the glassy ice; the thought brought warmth to my soul.

"Priscilla, there's a pet store!" I excitedly exclaimed as the *Pawesome Pooch* store came and went. "I bet a sweater from there would cost me a good chunk of my salary," I mumbled, smiling and rolling my eyes at the thought of how Priscilla liked expensive things. She seemed to know the difference between wool and acrylic.

A large, flashing digital billboard advertising the Winter Games flashed a photo of a handsome cowboy and then showed a promo photo of him skijoring with a cowboy hat. "Hello, *cowboy*," I mumbled, making my last turn before the chalet. "They just make them different up here in Wyoming," I giggled, reminiscing about that cowboy's rugged jawline.

"You have arrived at your destination," my GPS screamed into the abyss of silence in my car. I yelped back out of fright, as I was deep in thought, contemplating *cowboys at a ski resort*, which further annoyed Priscilla for interrupting her beauty sleep.

The luxury chalet row was incredible, just off the main road for the resort in a line of many individual chalets, all managed by the same company. A fleeting thought of wonder passed my mind for who owned them. I pulled up my Yukon to the chalet that I reserved, with a large "2" hanging on the downstairs door. The smell of pine trees was intoxicating; I could practically hear the crackling of logs in the fire. I left my skis outside the front door in a snow mound, grabbed my bags and ski boots, and after a quick potty break for Priscilla outside, I punched in the code for the front door and was greeted by a stunning floorplan.

Light hardwood floors, tan wood beams on the ceiling, and a grand chandelier hanging over the extra-plush sectional couch. A beautiful off-white kitchen with glistening granite countertops had all gold finishes and hardware. Floor to ceiling windows gave the most remarkable view of a snowy pine tree forest, with a hint of Sage Mountain's chairlifts in the distance. The corners of the windows were delicately frosted from the cold. It was like living in a snow globe in the dreamiest winter wonderland. I kicked off my shoes. As Priscilla started roaming around, I wondered why I hadn't thought of this sooner.

An hour later, following a mad case of the zoomies, Priscilla was snoring in her bed in front of the gas fireplace. She was bouncing off the walls just moments ago, which was adorable to watch. We even played fetch for a bit, though she found running around the coffee table more interesting than her toys I brought from home. I had a fresh mug of hot cocoa—the real kind made from milk and chocolate—and it was *divine,* while I clicked on the television to see another weather report.

"Record breaking snowfall expected at Sage Mountain Resort this weekend! But unless you pow chasers are already there, your luck may be up, as the highway is expected to close down. Snowplow crews are already running on overdrive as they gear up for the Winter Games, so don't expect a fast turnaround on opening back up, either." I turned it back off. Good thing I brought groceries for the week, though now that I was there, my appetite was craving way more carbs than I came prepared for. It was still early, not yet dark, and the snow hadn't started yet. I decided a last-minute trip to the store for supplies was a good idea.

Jumping up from the couch, Priscilla got her second wind for the day, looking at me as if to ask, "Where are we going?" I checked the mirror; just because I was happy in my singledom, didn't mean I want to look ragged in public, right? My brown hair was shiny, thanks to my last-minute appointment for a blowout yesterday. My green eyes popped with this moody taupe eyeshadow, and the cheeks were naturally flushed because of the warm cocoa. My outfit, a 2-piece tan jogger set was okay, but not really giving "ski holiday." Priscilla looked more the part than I did in her cute, green sweater with white snowflakes embroidered on it. I decided a quick outfit change into a beige turtleneck sweater, dark jeans, and snow boots would be much cuter. I put a black headband in my hair, pushing the hair out of my face. It worked. I felt *cute.* And that was enough for me.

As Priscilla and I walked to the car, off in the distance I saw a man walking a horse into a barn. The sight seemed unusual for the area, but I realized it must have been part of the skijoring that I had heard so much about on the way up there. I smirked; after all of the ads I heard, I felt like an expert on the matter. The first snowflake fell on my windshield as I got back out onto the road. The coziness of the incoming storm was exciting me to no end.

Pushing the cart around *Natural Grocers,* with Priscilla in the child seat, we made several bad decisions. The first of which, we hit the ice cream aisle. Then, we got some bacon to sizzle up in the morning, mostly because I wanted her to have a treat, too, since she wasn't about to have a bite of my Rocky Road. Next, I got a variety of ready-made food. Lastly, I stocked up on colorful pastas, fresh mozzarella, and aged Parmesan cheese. I decided to skip the garlic bread since I had ice cream. Balance.

The woman at the checkout had long, bright red nails that matched her sweater. She was chewing gum at high speed, popping it every few seconds. Her nails clicking on every packaged item that she scanned was entertaining.

"And how are you girls doing tonight?" she asked, gum popping erratically, beaming at me in between.

"We're good! Preparing for the storm. And you?"

"Oh yeah, you and everyone else getting ready for the weather. It's '*no carb left behind*' around here. If there's a single box left of mac and cheese at the end of my shift, it will be a miracle." She winked, and I considered just how good macaroni sounded.

As we left the store, the flakes started falling faster. By the time we got back to the chalet, it was nearly pitch black and a full-blown blizzard. Priscilla wasn't happy about her last potty outside for the evening, as the snow was up to her chest, but thankfully I brought her snow booties and heavy winter coat that protected her fur from getting wet.

Back in the chalet, Priscilla and I each ate our dinner—hers of the finest quality refrigerated dog food that looks like human grade eats—and mine, a lovely chicken carbonara pasta for one. In my coziest plush pajamas, we made our way to the bedroom, where normally, I would read for a few hours in my winding down time. But no reading on this trip, unless it was the Bible, which I enjoyed for thirty minutes before turning off the lights and falling asleep.

*****

I awoke to a freezing house. Priscilla was pressed up against me under the covers, body burrowed into the blankets. Slipping on a pair of thick socks and a heavy robe that was left for me next to the soaking tub, I went downstairs to investigate.

Finding the thermostat, I cranked it up to a toasty seventy degrees. I also turned on the gas fireplace to warm up the chalet faster, as I walked past the wood burning stove. I opened the latch—no wood inside, or I'd have lit that, too. I remembered seeing a stack of wood outside by the driveway. It was barely past dawn; I went back to bed, the warmth rising to the loft quickly.

We slept for two more hours. I never slept in at home; with work being early and running late into the evenings with books I brought home, I had never realized how hard on my sleeping pattern that was. The stacks of manuscripts that surrounded me were always looming over my head. Since I'd been free of them for 24 hours, I felt their power waning. They could wait. This trip was about me.

Getting out of bed, I slipped my feet into the sherpa slippers that I kicked off last night next to the king-size beauty sleep machine. Doing a few stretches, I felt great. The mattress was an upgrade to mine at home, and I considered slipping off the sheets to see what the make was when I felt another chill in the air. Throwing on my robe and tightening it, I reached for Priscilla, who let out a groan.

"Time to get up, sleepy head," I said in a coo, but it didn't work, as she let out the faintest growl when I went to move her. "Okay, up, Priscilla." That worked, as she did know that command. "Let's go potty outside. After that? You can sleep all day, if you want. Because mommy's going skiing." I looked out the window and felt the excitement in my bones. The snowstorm came through, and it absolutely *dumped* overnight.

The walk from the chalet to the new gondola was as advertised; less than 100 yards. In my barely-worn black ski pants that made a delightful *swoosh* with every step I took, black turtleneck and fitted white ski jacket, I felt cool. Stylish. *Sleek.* I was glad for it, as carrying my skis over my shoulder became cumbersome after about three steps.

The lines were miraculously short as I raced to ride the new gondola at the base of Sage Mountain. Peering over to the other chair lifts, the crowds were easily 2–3 times in size. Looking at the base map, I realized why: This gondola went to easier runs, whereas the lifts went to more challenging peaks for which I was more than pleased with. I was a good skier, but I enjoyed wide, groomed trails. I wasn't trying to overdo anything on my first trip skiing in years.

The singles line meant that I got to cut even more people, since I didn't care about riding with a particular group. I was on the second gondola of the morning, and the ride up was filled with chatter, excitement, and peering out the window as we crossed a deep canyon filled with snowy trees and off-piste trails. Six people in total were in the gondola, and I was sitting directly across from a man, but I couldn't see anything definitive about his appearance. His goggles were down, and he was in head to toe black, other than a tiger face mask. The gondola slowed, as it usually did if someone needed extra time at the top, and the slightest movement of his hand revealed the skin on his wrist. In certain cultures, showing skin on the wrist would be considered scandalous. I smirked at the thought and was about to be bold enough to ask him about the mask when I was interrupted by someone in the gondola pointing out a moose.

"Look—right there! There's a *huge* momma moose," one woman said.

"I hope I don't run into her or her babies while I'm skiing," another woman said, with an undertone of fear in her voice. I hadn't thought of that possibility, and too, felt worried.

"Just stay on the trails and you'll be fine. No off-roading, okay?" The man next to her put his arm around her for reassurance. She nodded.

"Are you watching the Winter Games this weekend?" a man asked the couple in front of them, as they still kept their gaze on the tall, overpowering animal.

"Just the skijoring," the man said, taking his arm back from around the woman's shoulders as we neared the top. "I have never seen it before, and I'm from a rodeo town. But we never get enough snow to do anything remotely as cool."

"Yeah, same. That Ford Prescott is something else." The conversationalist next to me let out a low whistle after he spoke, emphasizing on Ford's name.

"And he's not bad to look at, either," the woman next to me spoke out, and the other woman laughed in agreement, her partner giving her a look. "What? I'm married, but I'm not *dead,*" she smirked. Ford Prescott... Was that the handsome cowboy I saw on the billboard, with a steely jaw, chin dimple, and yesterday's stubble? Maybe I would have to watch the games after all.

When we reached the top, I felt my ears pop with the change in elevation. I was the first to get out, and since the gondola never stops moving, I felt the pressure of retrieving my skis from their holder as quickly as possible, as I skirted around it in my ski boots. A small ice patch nearly took me down in the process, but I caught myself and walked out of the way so I could put them on and analyze my route.

Once I was out and in the place where everyone put their skis on, the man in the tiger mask flew past me on his powder skis. He was a very good skier, which was obvious.

Standing below the map was an older ski host, armed with a solo ski pole as his pointer, so he could advise people on which runs to take. He was at least a decade older than me, if not more, and I wasn't even done putting on my skis yet when he struck up a conversation.

"Good morning. What kind of adventure are you seeking today?" His blue eyes sparkled as he spoke. There was a softness to him, a dad-vibe that I found endearing.

"A mid-level adventure, at least to start. I'm afraid the number of years I've been off skis are rivaling the years I have," I said as I clicked into my skis, putting my poles under my arm and taking in the map. The options of ski runs were endless, with everything from family learning zones to triple blacks. I decided to be a little more specific. "I'd like to stick to groomers, if possible. I'm over the age of awareness; I'm not trying to ski moguls if I can help it." He let out a laugh, nodding.

"Of course. I'm well past my mogul years, too. How about this route—" He pointed to a blue run that broke off into every which way. "Start out on 'Shadow Dancer,' then turn right into 'Gimmicks,' keep right as the trails merge with 'Potato Chip,' and then it's imperative you take the cat track right here—that will be immediately to your left—called 'Snickering Kitty,' and you take that run for just a moment before it opens up to the best, blue groomer we have, all the way back here. Otherwise, you'll be heading for a double black mogul field called 'Blackbeard's Revenge.'"

"Shadow… Potato Chip… Kitty?" I mumbled, my head scrambling to remember the route. "Seriously, who names these runs?"

"Have fun!" he exclaimed before moving down the map to help another group of skiers who were scratching their heads at the map.

"Shadow, Potato Chip, Kitty." I said it three more times as I pulled my goggles over my helmet, tightening everything in the back. The faintest clouds were in the sky as I looked over to the starting point, where the mountain sloped off just-so. Taking a huge gulp of fresh, alpine air, I felt rejuvenated. Free. *Alive.* "Thank you, Lord, for bringing me here. I pray for a fun time, safety, and only groomed runs." Smiling, I took off on "Shadow Dancer," slowly making a few wide turns before finding my ski legs and tightening my pattern in the freshly laid snow that sparkled in the sunlight. By the time I got to my first crossroads, I had forgotten the words I'd been repeating. I slowed, stopping in a fluid movement and spraying snow in the process.

"Hockey Puck, Gimmicks, or Ruffles?" I read the signs aloud; two of which were blue and the other, Ruffles, was snow covered, so I couldn't see its rating. One was left, one was straight, and the other was right. I couldn't for the life of me recall anything other than Potato Chip and Kitty. "Oh, Potato Chip—maybe he was speaking in *code,*" I said, shaking my head as I headed straight down on Ruffles. What could go wrong?

At the end of the run, that I had to take in full blown "pizza" formation—my legs were so wide, it looked like I was playing a school yard game of London Bridge—my limbs felt like gelatin. I was sore and tired as I dodged the moguls and did everything I could to keep control of my turns with a steep grade I wasn't ready for. I wasn't certain, but I had a feeling that it was the wrong run.

I managed to find a moderate cat track that looped down quite a bit of the mountain before reaching a cluster of blue runs and successfully avoided mogul fields. I ended up going back up the gondola three more times, as I couldn't get enough of the amazing conditions. My turns down the mountain powder felt like frosting in a wedding cake. In the morning, its softness made it easier to warm up, and by mid-day, the snow had formed an upper crust from the cold that made my turns feel sharper with better execution. If it wasn't for my bladder, my stomach, and my muscles alerting me that it was enough for the day, I would have stayed out here until the last chair.

Getting back to the chalet, Priscilla was thrilled to see me. It appeared her energy levels from being cooped up inside were finally recovering from her lazy day yesterday, and she was ready for some serious play time. If we were home, I would have taken her out to our covered dog area at the condos, but since we were here, and there was a foot and a half of snow outside, I ended up throwing a toy for her to fetch for nearly fifteen minutes before she had her fill.

We ended the day with a nice dinner, consisting of a few things I picked up at the grocery store, including Sage Mountain's highest quality macaroni pasta from a local pasta maker and a cup of tea, before my eyes slammed shut in the cozy king bed upstairs, where I had the most restful sleep of my life.

Waking early the next morning, Priscilla, too, seemed extra rested, having the zoomies as we traipsed downstairs to fill her food dish. She excitedly ate while I showered and dressed for another day on the slopes.

I decided to warm up for the day with a nice cup of hot chocolate. After starting my mug of milk in the microwave, the power surged, going out. "Oh no," I said, with Priscilla even feeling that something wasn't right about that. When it came back on ten seconds later, I restarted the microwave. "Hope that doesn't happen again." I was stirring the chocolate into my hot milk, already forgetting it when it happened a second time. But unlike the first, the power didn't immediately come back on. I traipsed over to my purse, digging for my phone. Service was extremely limited out here, and I'd had it turned off to not be distracted by it, but it appeared I'd forgotten to plug it in because it was completely dead. "That's okay,'" I told myself. "Don't panic." I looked out the windows towards town. Plenty of lights were on in the community; as the sun was just rising and I could see clearly, it wasn't like an EMP or something. Gah, I'd read one too many apocalypse novels to be dealing with this alone at the moment. *Don't let the intrusive thoughts win, Presley.* But the lights from Sage Mountain were comforting, and I saw the chair lifts in the distance. A reminder I was at a heavily populated resort that very likely had generators. It was quite possible it was just my chalet that lost electricity. However, I had no phone, no power, no Wi-Fi, and no way of getting help—unless, of course, I went out into the freezing temps and found it. As I looked back outside, I saw the snow was falling once again.

After several minutes of wrestling with what to do, I decided I would wait it out. I had a wood burning stove, after all. Ready-to-eat food in the fridge. The only thing that absolutely required electricity was my charger. All I needed was wood. Besides, Priscilla needed to go for a potty break anyway. Someone had been by to shovel the walks and the driveway this morning around my car, or the walks were heated, which made more sense. This place was fancy like that. It was safe, and everything was perfectly accessible. So, we bundled up—her in her pink puffer jacket with little rhinestone accents and her snow boots that she absolutely despised—and me, in my white ski jacket. I was wearing my ski clothes already except for shoes, so I threw on some snow boots. Holding Priscilla's leash, I let her extend it as far as she needed to go while I headed for the wood pile, letting the door shut behind me. I grabbed as many logs as I could comfortably hold and waited for Priscilla to sniff every part of the earth. When she was done, we walked back to the front door.

Entering the code, the buttons made no noise. Hmm. I hit "Enter," but nothing happened. What—is this door somehow hard wired into the electricity? I tried it three more times. A cold wind shifted in my direction—my knees started to tremble. Dropping the wood, I picked up Priscilla who was also shivering. "I'm sorry sweetie. It appears we're *locked out.*" Ugh. It must have been connected to Wi-Fi!! How did I not consider that before going out there? It was eerily reminiscent of how every episode of *Dateline* starts. The narrator's voice boomed in my head. *"Presley Astor thought this was just like every other ski trip. . . She was wrong."* Now what? I looked around at the row of chalets, as I considered my options.

Priscilla's Inner Monologue

Splendid. We've been cast into the cold. Just try not to trip as you carry me through the snow, darling.

CHAPTER 2: FORD
BLIZZARD PREP & BAD PRESS

The last five reps were the hardest of the set; it took everything I had in me to put the barbell back on its rack as I finished up my bench presses. I was covered in sweat and reaching for my towel as my phone started to ring, *again.* Checking the caller ID, I sent it to voicemail without another thought.

The third bedroom in my chalet made for a perfect gym: a few weight racks, a bench, and a treadmill kept me strong. Being raised on a cattle ranch and coming from a long line of strong, stocky men, I noticed from a young age that I had greater natural strength than most of my peers. Though I was far from a ranch life now, I couldn't just sit idly. I needed to move and work my muscles.

For skijoring, while your body has to be strong to maintain control as you whip around the turns of the tracks, the biggest strength comes from your arms and hands. The ability to maintain the rope hold is crucial; but you have to be able to work the rope, knowing when to give slack and adjust angles as you make your way around the track at breakneck speeds.

Not once did I ever consider that the sport would have taken me this far. Everything I had was from skijoring prize money, brand partnerships, and collaborations. I started skijoring when I was nine years old. Me and a few other ranch kids in the area would go to empty campgrounds in the winter where we'd build a track and jumps. Friends of their families would bring horses or snowmobiles to pull us around, while most of the adults just enjoyed the bonfire and socializing. Often, I'd ask whoever was pulling me to go as fast as the horse or machine could go in the conditions so I could practice. The other kids couldn't keep up with me.

When I started entering the peewee divisions at the local rodeo circuits and winning, I kept up with it. Now, I've traveled all over the Rockies for skijoring. My manager even got me a short trip to Europe a few years ago. I could have kept going like this for the foreseeable future and had a great time. But I had a secret. At the end of that month, my manager's contract was up. We renewed it every two years; and he had no reason to think this year would be any different. Except it was in every way. I had my eyes set on another goal: retiring from the sport.

Since my fiancé ended things with me last year, after revealing she'd been having an emotional affair with the CEO of Sage Mountain Ski Resort, Trent Langley, I'd trudged on. I didn't let it break me. Poppy and I had been together for twelve months, engaged after only ten weeks of dating. The engagement was as much her idea as it was my manager's; the "family man image got more deals these days than heartthrob," his words exactly. Truthfully, I didn't need much nudging. Poppy was everything to me. I put her on a pedestal, weaving in and out of the red flags she casually put out, like a slalom race course. . . And there were many. Still, I believed she was the "one" that God had sent in my path.

Now, I had been having a really hard time connecting to God when I did everything I could to force His hand by getting in a relationship with a woman like that, and it only caused me to crash and burn. The hardest part? The dog that Poppy talked me into getting during our engagement—she took it when we broke up. My heart was broken twice, losing both my fiancé and my little buddy, an Australian shepherd named Toby. Sure, Wyoming ranchers are built differently from your average city folk, but all the strength in the world didn't prepare me for the feelings I was dealing with now, like betrayal and losing my dog. On top of it all, I felt like I was losing my spiritual strength.

Every time I tried to talk to God about my feelings, I hit a wall. I was drowning in regret. Embarrassment. Shame. I wanted God to cleanse me of these feelings, but I just felt so wounded. Honestly, I was ready to move on. I was ready to let go. But with that dark cloud looming over my sport, and words traveling faster than a lubed up inner tube on a Black Diamond, I felt I'd guarded my heart and mind once again. This time, I wouldn't be so quick to let anyone break through those walls.

My favorite thing about my new chalet here in Sage Mountain, other than its proximity to a great horse boarding facility that had a large barn for my horses, was that no one except my manager knew exactly where I was. Of course, it was known that I had a home here and was based at this resort over winters. Heck, it was listed on my Wikipedia page that I was here. After my breakup with Poppy, I sold my home and had this one built on land I'd bought years ago. And, with all of the chalets around me being short-term rentals, often full of families just trying to get their kids' energy out on the slopes, I had managed to lay low so far. If someone was knocking on my door, it was a food delivery service and not someone who needed to speak with me. My phone buzzed again. I wished the same could be said about my phone number. I quickly hit "ignore."

My other favorite amenity about this chalet was the hundreds of ski trails just out my front door. The new gondola installed enabled me to take runs at my fancy without standing in line with most of the general public, who still favored the other chairs. But I didn't have as much time for skiing that season as I'd had liked. With the cheating scandal that was plaguing my sport and without knowing explicitly who had been involved, I opted to lay low that year, trading in my downhill recreational skis for my steady slalom racers I trained on. Besides, I got too much attention last year when it was revealed that Poppy left me for Trent Langley, and every once in a while, people still wanted to ask me questions about it.

Now, with the cheating scandal, I was afraid they might have asked more questions about the professional kind of cheating I may have witnessed, and I didn't think my mind could take it. I couldn't point a finger at my fellow competitors. My friends. Besides, I'd never even seen anything suspicious. So, if I was out in the snow on skis at all, I was at the training track. At least there, we had a strict athlete-only policy, and no press was allowed in. There, I was free from the questions and could focus on improving my speeds.

After a shower, I threw on some jeans and a thermal long-sleeve shirt. I had to go down to feed the horses later but until then, I wanted to get to the bottom of that rumor. If half the talk was true, riders were throwing races so that another competitor could win. First things first—I needed to talk to my manager.

"Ford—just the man the world is wanting to hear from. What do I owe the pleasure?" My manager, Jack, always an air for the dramatics, answered the phone.

"Good morning, Jack. I'm seeing a lot of things in the news, and I just want to keep my name clear. I haven't bribed any other riders to throw their races to get where I am. I just want to make that known."

"Relax, cowboy. So far, no one is associating any cheating to us, Ford. Unfortunately, I can't say that we don't know anyone who is. Remember your pal, Beau Perry? That's another story. He was seen chatting very closely with another competitor who just so happened to very awkwardly lose their race." I squeezed the bridge of my nose as Jack told me the news. Beau was more than a fellow racer to me there in Sage

Mountain—he was a friend. Last year, he boarded one of his horses with mine. The thought of him cheating was shattering.

"I'll give him the benefit of the doubt, but I sure hope he hasn't been involved in this scandal this whole time. Heck, he nearly whooped me on that last race of ours. If it wasn't for him wearing the extra-wide Slalom skis that didn't let him turn fast enough, I think he would've broken a world record." I started overanalyzing the memories of the race to make sure I had thought it through. Nothing was out of the ordinary that I could remember.

"That's my man. Ford, you're the first to not throw a stone. I admire you for that. I wish I could say the same about some of the other athletes that didn't make the Winter Games. Like Jace Kelly. It looks like his social media team has been hired by a prosecutor for Beau Perry. Not a single second spared throwing him under the bus."

Grimacing at the thought, I was reminded that some athletes had an inability to keep to themselves. But, at the same time, it did feel like a betrayal to learn that someone you competed against maybe wasn't playing fair.

"We'll never know for Beau, it seems. He's decided to take a leave of absence from the sport. Probably get a retirement announcement before too long from him. He was already having knee problems, after all." I wished I knew what Jack thought of that, since it was exactly what I was planning to do, too.

"Thanks, Jack, for the information. Beau is a friend, and I wish him well," I mumbled.

"Either way, this problem isn't ours. Our association is long overdue for setting regulations for things like this, and sometimes, it's the unfortunate circumstances like these that force their hand to do so," Jack said.

"Hey, I better get going. There's some catastrophic storm hitting the mountain tonight, and I need to get my horses situated."

"I did see the numbers for the storm. Should be a great weekend with all that fresh powder. I can't wait to see you race, Ford." *If only I could go out and ski it without being questioned by every reporter known to man.*

"It will be. And they are going to be working around the clock to groom the racetrack for our competition." I peered out the window at the training arena not too far off. The best thing for me was to keep my head out of the drama and focus on the game.

"Don't talk to any reporters. I think it's best that we keep your name out of the paper, lest they come sniffing you out and distracting you during your training. I know you have nothing to hide, Ford. Let's just stay focused and keep anything associated with your name as the driver to buy tickets, not to investigate. This will die down. Sadly, while it seems a huge deal to us, there's nothing anyone can do about *past* allegations. Only the current suspicions, and right now, everyone is behaving like a perfect angel. It will blow over before the games. I mean it."

"I agree. If I wanted my name in the paper, I would buy the entire front page of the *New York Times.*" We hung up, and I felt relieved to not be associated with any more drama than I already was.

The day went by as expected. Giant storm incoming, frantic skiers trying to get there despite the roads threatening to close, and all of the chalets in the row of mine were certainly booked up. I expected to start seeing guests arriving by the handfuls. But that far, only the one next to me appeared to be occupied, as I saw the car pull into the driveway. Before I could see who got out, my computer chimed. I grudgingly went to see what it was, expecting it to be a request for an interview. I was pleasantly surprised that my favorite ski brand wanted to do a partnership deal. I let out a huge sigh of relief; that was what I needed to distract me from everything else I had going on.

I weighed the pros and cons, considering my upcoming retirement decision: Would agreeing to take a deal in light of what was to come of my career be misleading? I looked at the offer again; there was nothing in it regarding skijoring. In fact, it was a brand that made the best of the best powder skis. They didn't want Ford Prescott the skijoring champion; they wanted Ford Prescott the cowboy skier. The proposed partnership included pictures of me on skis, on a snowy mountain, wearing head to toe denim and a cowboy hat. It was actually a really fun premise, and I decided to go for it.

After I let Jack know that I was interested in the ski partnership, I went out to my kitchen to make an afternoon pick me up; a strong cup of coffee. It didn't matter what time of day or night; I could slam enough caffeine to power a freight train and still sleep soundly. It was a gift that I didn't take for granted, as I loved a nice, dark brew with rich, earthy notes and just a splash of raw cream. It was how we used to drink coffee on the ranch in Big Horn, Wyoming where I grew up, and there wasn't a day that went by that I didn't recall the memories fondly.

Taking my brew to the window, I saw the woman who I assumed was my neighbor for the week. She was lugging bags over her shoulder and placing a pair of *Stockli* skis out in the snow. *She has excellent taste,* I thought, as I wondered where her husband was to carry all that heavy stuff in for her? Then, I saw it: a fluffy, beige dog in a bright green sweater, marking its territory in the white snow. From here, I couldn't quite make it out, but it appeared that the dog was wearing two tufts of hair on her head like pigtails. A smile crossed my face, immediately shaken off. *Stay focused, Ford.* I can't afford any distractions right now. Or ever, for that matter. As the clouds started to roll in, I knew I better get to the horses.

If it wasn't for the tinted windows on my white Ram 3500 truck, it might have blended into the snow. I supposed the fact that it was covered in sand from the town of Sage Mountain, furiously working to prevent a tourist sliding into another car, helped my case, too. After arriving at the barn and arena, I scanned my card to get in the security gate. Inside, my horses Whiskey, Buckshot, and Outlaw ran up to inspect the pockets on my jacket for carrots or horse cubes.

"Hold your horses, guys." I smirked at my own joke. "I have plenty for everyone." All of them seem to have a talent for the dramatics. I pulled out a bag of long carrots and started handing them out as I gave everyone a quick inspection. "Who wants some fresh air?" I turned to open the gate of their corral, and they quickly ran out the barn doors. The only thing my horses loved more than carrots was fresh snow; they'd been like that since they were colts. Curious and playful. And I bought them each based on that fact. "Tonight, we're getting lots of fresh powder," I told them, as they stretched their legs, not a single one acknowledging my words. Whiskey and Buckshot ran back in to get a drink from the trough, as Outlaw came back over to me to see about another carrot.

Off in the distance, I saw movement at the chalets. The woman that was my neighbor was holding something under her arm like a football; I surmised it was the dog, now wearing a pink bodysuit of some kind. I looked away, an annoyed smirk forming on my lips. "Tourists," I mumbled under my breath. "Say what you want about them, but they are entertaining," I said to Outlaw, who couldn't care less about my words, just wanted the carrots in my hand. His velvety, wet nose tickled my skin as he gobbled up the last of them.

Back home, I was seasoning a ribeye steak when I got a news alert on my phone. Somehow, the technology on my phone thought that I wanted to know when articles from every armpit of the internet mentioned my name. I glanced at it, not reading the headline, but seeing the image was of my ex, Poppy, and her boyfriend, Trent. She was wearing a white veil, white dress, and he was in a tuxedo. I pushed the phone away, underestimating my own strength. It slid off the counter onto the hardwood floor, shattering the screen. A feeling of relief washed over me: if my phone was broken, I had a very good reason to ignore everyone coming my way. I powered it off, screen unreadable, and the phone went dark. I'd send Jack an email tomorrow morning that I'd be out of touch until further notice, but for that night, I'd be there, trying not to think about the fact that Poppy was married, and how that article somehow mentioned me in passing.

That door had been closed for quite some time. Despite nearly a year passing since she spoke those relationship-killing words, "I'm in love with someone else," I hadn't found a reason to put myself back out there.

It hadn't been because of a lack of interest, I was blessed to say. I'd had several women contact me for dating but called me old fashioned—I wanted to be the one who pursues the woman. In this day and age of everything being online, that was challenging, but I'd opted out of online dating or social media profiles of any kind. I wanted to lay low and let things happen naturally.

Naturally. A year or more ago, I would have scoffed at that thought. I did everything I could to win Poppy's attention, and she was nothing but mind games. The relationship wasn't ordained by God in the slightest. *Sigh.* There I went again, reliving past hurts. I considered praying. An urge that hadn't passed me in quite some time. But the moment I closed my eyes, I started thinking about the shame of my past choices once again, and I felt further from God than ever.

A long time ago, I read a verse about when we repent, God forgives our mistakes and never thinks of them again. Yet, I couldn't figure out how God could forgive me when I couldn't even forgive myself.

The snowflakes started to fall steadily, and I watched them from my favorite picture window. My chalet had the best view out of the whole row; they all backed up to an aspen grove, but mine had a small creek that moose would frequent. Each chalet had some elbow room—a requirement for anywhere I live is that I not be on top of my neighbors, since I was used to living on a ranch in rural Wyoming. No, these chalets were good, I thought. A swift knock at the door plucked me out of my gaze.

My favorite thing about the twenty-first century is contactless grocery delivery. Sure, I missed the days when I could go into a store and shop without being recognized. These days, it went so much further. Everyone assumed that since they recognized my face or bought a sponsored product, they had untethered access to me with no boundaries required. I may be a rough and tough Wyoming born and raised cowboy, but I also have feelings. They were just deeply recessed at the moment.

I put away my bags of groceries and plucked a pint of vanilla ice cream out of the freezer to thaw for dessert. I would end the night as I always did, watching a movie that reminded me of something that brought me calm, usually an old western, and trying to avoid everything else that didn't.

The next morning, I awoke to my favorite childhood pastime: an abundance of snow, covering every surface with its thick, heavy powder. It looked like a blanket had been put out over the entire resort. Suddenly, my feet felt an itch to ski that I could barely ignore. The runs were going to be fantastic today. I reached for my phone to check the snow gauges before remembering it was broken, while I wrestled with the decision if I wanted to risk being recognized. I thought I could wear my helmet with the most coverage. But that wouldn't cover up my very distinct chin dimple or scar on my jaw. My black jacket that zipped up over my chin would be an option. But what if it slipped? Then, it dawned on me: I had a half-face gator with a cheesy tiger face on it that I got at a white elephant party last year. That was the perfect disguise for me to enjoy my ski day.

It took me a minute to find skis that I hadn't done a product deal with, as those pairs had my name engraved on them as a gift from the company. Sorting through my garage, I found a pair of Atomic skis that I got as a graduation gift nearly a decade ago. They were barely used powder skis, and just what I needed for all of this fresh snow. Stepping out of my chalet, I saw my neighbor leaving a few moments before me. I held back just a second, mostly so I didn't end up in a conversation.

Coincidentally, my neighbor—whom I reminded myself did not know I'd seen her, who I was, or that it was me under this mask—she and I ended up in the same bright red gondola. The second one of the day, I admired her commitment to skiing. The rest of the group was chatting eagerly, and I attempted to hold my breath when my name was brought up, lest someone realize I was sitting right there. I just sat still, not trying to get anyone's attention. As I sat across from my neighbor, I couldn't help but notice how beautiful she was. Her thick, brown hair was braided on one side and poking out of her white helmet: the fleeting brightness of the sun revealing golden hues. Her goggles, pulled up on her helmet, were bright purple, which added some much-needed color on a snowy day like today. But it was her icy blue eyes that gripped me. As we reached the top, I saw her shiny lips smirking at something. If it had been just us and no other riders who definitely knew who I was, I would've asked her what was funny. But for now, I let it go.

I couldn't get out of the gondola soon enough. Every time I closed my eyes, I kept seeing her; a vision I didn't want nor need for distraction. This woman was trouble with a capital T, and I would do everything in my power to avoid her. I just needed to get through this storm and the Winter Games.

Skiing was the adrenaline rush I didn't know I needed. As I carved through the tougher and ungroomed territory, I found few people on the same trails with me. The clouds gave way to the most beautiful blue skies and for a moment, I lifted my goggles and pulled down the neck gator and felt the warmth on my face. Two snowboarders came ripping up behind me where I was stopped mid-trail—an etiquette of being out on the slopes that you'd never want to break—so I quickly moved off to the side, hoping they didn't stop to see me or to talk. They didn't. I released my breath.

Call me paranoid, but when your sport is the biggest news story on all of the major news networks, and I'd been fortunate to be considered the face of Skijoring, it doesn't feel good to be constantly stopped and questioned. Especially with my ex-fiancé getting married and my name being brought up in such articles; I just wanted to lay low.

With a zest of joy and tired legs, I finished the day a few minutes before the last chair, and instead of taking the gondola, I skied down a back way and came out near my horses. A farm gate was the only thing keeping me from being able to ski all the way to my house from there; one that I didn't have a key to. So, after unclipping my skis and awkwardly filling the corral with hay via pitchfork in my ski boots, I made sure the horses had fresh water in their trough and walked the rest of the way home with my skis slung over my shoulder. The snowflakes were starting to ramp up again, and since I was no longer moving at high speeds as I worked my way down mountain trails, the cold caught up to me. By the time I reached my chalet, I could barely punch the numbers into my garage keypad to throw my skis inside.

Peeling off a few layers of my ski clothes, I left my black henley undershirt and ski pants on while I threw a few logs into my wood stove. Call me old fashioned, but I can't stand gas fireplaces. There's something that I find incredibly wrong about having a fire started with the click of a button. Sure, everything else in my chalet was top of the line—just like the other nine in this row of ten. But this was something I couldn't budge on, and I didn't let them put that faux-wood monstrosity in there. Stoking the roaring fire, it began to crank out the heat, so I went to the kitchen and figured out what I could make. The grocery delivery brought so many options, but I didn't really feel like cooking; rather, something fast. Lazy. So, I made a sandwich.

I was halfway done with the meal when the power began flickering. Stopping my bite mid-chew, I waited a few moments, and it came back on. I finished my ham and cheese when it went off again. The beeping of my generator was a relief; it kicked all of my power back on, gloriously shining throughout the house. I went around and flipped lights off, wanting to conserve what I could in the meantime. Looking out my front window, I saw a very unusual sight to the left of me; the woman from next door, grabbing bundles of wood that were stacked outside, while her little dog sniffed around the pavement. The dog on the leash was as far away from her as it could get before she motioned with her head for it to come back inside, to which the little dog minded and went back over to her. But they didn't go inside. She dropped the wood after a moment, picked up her dog, and disappeared.

Sitting on the couch, I thought of all the places she might have gone on foot with a little dog in a pink coat in this brewing storm and cold front. Before my phone broke, my weather app said tonight was going to reach record lows. Running my hands through my hair, I realized I needed to go out and see if this woman needed help. Every year, tourists get rescued from danger on this mountain, but tonight, it might have been happening right in my backyard. As I stood up to put my ski layers back on, a knock at the door caught me by surprise.

"I'm so sorry to bother you, but it appears that I'm locked out, and we are absolutely frigid cold right now. I see that your power is on. Do you think that I could perhaps come in and use your phone?" I was so caught off guard by the woman standing on my porch, holding a shivering dog, that I just nodded and let them in. It was the woman staying next door. The woman from the gondola ride. The woman who had been creeping into my thoughts ever since I saw her yesterday, and I didn't even know what to say right now.

"Of course," I mumbled. Then I remembered my phone was broken. "Except, uh, my phone is broken." I shut the door behind them to keep the heat in the house, when I saw her eyes look beyond me. I kept it unlocked, as I didn't want to put off any creepy vibes, and she nodded.

"Oh, okay then. Mine is inside my chalet. What should I do?" My mind was blank as she spoke. Did she say she was locked out?

"I, uh, have a key for the other chalets. Which one is yours?" Her eyes widened as I spoke.

"Why do *you* have a key to *my* rental?"

I was digging through my kitchen drawer when I found the keyring. "Long story."

Her jaw dropped. After a long pause, she mumbled something under her breath. "Okay, then." She looked at me with her arms crossed, still holding her dog. I could tell she was skeptical. Just waiting to jump down my throat with questions, but there was a hesitation. Finally, she relented, looking around my chalet. Mine, unlike the others, had rustic barnwood floors and ceilings. What no one ever talks about is how barnwood is the most expensive type of material you can get. I liked it because it reminded me of home on the ranch.

"I'm in chalet '2'," she said.

"Here you go. Do you want me to help you?" Chivalry isn't dead, but as soon as I said it, I wondered just what I would be helping her with.

"No, that's okay. I think I can manage." She smiled a radiant, toothy grin, took the key, and spun around on her heels. "I'm Presley, by the way. Here for the week. Hopefully, the power comes back on." *Presley.*

"Ford. Nice to meet you, Presley." She didn't turn back around. "If you need anything at all, I'll be here." This was entirely out of character for me, as I had been retreated from the entirety of civilization, but it didn't seem like Presley even knew who I was. And that was fine with me. Then, she stopped in her tracks.

"Wait! I know *you.*" A pit formed in my stomach at her words. Then, she pointed to the tiger gator on the hook near my front door. "You sat across from me in the gondola this morning." She grinned again, nearly taking me out with relief. "I was wondering who was under that mask. Well, I better go. Thanks, Ford." And with that, she was back outside, and the door shut behind her. The snow melting on my floors was the only sign she had been there at all. I caught myself going to the window at lightning speed to see if she made it back into her chalet next to mine, and she did.

"Get a grip, Ford. You have too much riding this weekend to be distracted by a woman. Not to mention, your decision about dating again." Talking to myself was a sure sign I'd been alone at home for too long. Now, with this neighbor situation? I was in trouble.

CHAPTER 3: PRESLEY
LOCKED OUT, LET IN

Knocking on a random door made me remember all of those true crime specials I watched late at night in college. Sure, the likelihood that someone in one of these chalets was a serial killer was low, but never *zero.* So, when the door opened to a little old lady looking in my direction, I was relieved.

"Hello, dear," she said, with an endearing southern accent.

"Hi, I'm so sorry to bother you, but I've just been locked out of my chalet. Do you possibly have a phone I could use?" Her eyes widened as she shook her head.

"No, I'm afraid not. I've managed to not keep up with technology, much to my children's chagrin. My kids are still out on the slopes. They have one, if you'd like to come inside and wait? I have the fire going. If your little one can wait outside, that is. I'm deathly allergic, I'm afraid." As she pointed at

Priscilla, I didn't bother with a spiel about her being more hypoallergenic than most dogs. I certainly wasn't looking to impose, nor was I willing to keep Priscilla outside. I looked down to the rest of the chalets. I thought I'd start with number one, to see if anyone could help me, but I still had eight more.

"That's okay. I might come back if I can't find one sooner," I said, giving her a smile. She reciprocated the gesture and shut the door, and Priscilla and I chugged on.

Trudging through the snow that separated the chalets, I considered my options. If someone wasn't in the rest of these with a phone ready to use, I could walk to the nearest business and see about using their phone. But, when I got said phone, who was I going to call? I hadn't thought that one through. I'd have to remember the name of my property management company I booked through. Was it *Mountain Chalet's* or *Chalets in the Mountains?* Groaning, I realized I'd have to ask them to look up a few sites so I could confirm even which one it was. Once again, my insecurities and trauma of being called "too much" by the last few years of dates—which admittedly were few—came back into play. I had been trying my hardest to tiptoe around people, lest they caught on to my reputation.

The truth? I didn't think I was too much of anything. I was successful in my career, inquisitive, and creative, but why did that mean I must become a doormat for men to wipe their feet on, so that they didn't feel less than? I just didn't believe God created me with my gifts and abilities to be putting them away whenever a man came around. Ugh.

Shaking off my past, I handed it over to God as I stepped onto the cleared driveway of the next chalet. "Lord, I am perfectly content with Your love. I do not need a man to fulfill me."

As I peered up at chalet three, a glow from inside and a humming of a generator told me this chalet was prepared for an outage. It gave off an amber glow like a lantern in this blizzard. I excitedly knocked on the door. But nothing could prepare me for the handsome jawline that opened the door.

It was *him*—the cowboy from the billboards. I was certain of it. That stubble, that jawline—the scar on his face. He was drop-dead gorgeous, and there I was, mumbling about needing help. I took in his looks; he had dark brown hair that was long enough to run his fingers through, but short enough that it was manly. Several inches taller than me; I'd guess he was six feet tall. He relented, and I was inside, dripping wet snow over his beautiful, barnwood floors. *Oh, these puppies are heated, too. He has good taste.*

Ford, as he introduced himself, told me his phone was broken. There was a real epidemic of phones around these chalets! Was Sage Mountain where smart phones came to die? While contemplating this, I got momentarily lost in his chestnut eyes. It was so warm and toasty in there, I found myself starting to not care when he said he had a key to *my* rented chalet. Why, why, why? I had so many questions, but—I stopped myself. That was usually where I got into the danger zone, and people wrote me off before they even knew me. Wait. Why did I care? Was it not just thirty seconds ago I told God I was perfectly content?

His chalet was a little more. . . rustic. Personalized. I realized this chalet wasn't a rental, but he owned it. If *my* chalet was "alpine chic," this was "ranch *rich,*" I decided. I wondered if he lived in it full time? Was he single or married? I didn't see a ring on his finger, not that I was interested. I reminded myself and God, as I was constantly clueing Him into my every thought, but just for the sake of knowledge. I did work in publishing, after all. Heck, I might write a book of my own one day and this could be prime information, whether or not this handsome—err, *the most gorgeous man I'd ever seen up close,* was available.

Available or not, he certainly didn't seem emotionally available. His words were few, but there was a kindness to him. A stillness. Maybe *a water that ran deep*, if you will. Exactly the type of man that I repelled with my every move. My thoughts went back to Parker, a guy I went on two dates with. One more date than usual. He told me I was beautiful and brought me flowers. I thought, *this could be it.* But by the end of the date, he said being around me was akin to experiencing the Spanish Inquisition. How was I supposed to know that I couldn't ask questions about the movie he picked out for us to watch on his backyard projector? I just wanted to know the name, who the actors were, and the year it was made. Was this popcorn from a bag? I tried to avoid seed oils. Who did the landscaping? It was nice but needed a strand of twinkle lights. Back to the movie, I may have looked up the filming location when he lost his mind. Turned the movie off. I was hurt, but shocked at his true colors. The man went from sweet and kind to angry and short tempered. I was relieved that I found out when I did rather than months down the road.

Now, as I stood before this hunk of a cowboy, I kept my pain to myself and let our encounter be short lived. No lollygagging. No loitering of any kind.

It was when I turned to leave, with the key to my chalet in hand, that I noticed the tiger mask hanging from a hook, and the words were out of my mouth before I could control it. I could feel the energy in the room change as if he was cringing that I was still here. But he was sitting across from me in the gondola that morning. Now I knew why he was wearing the disguise—he was quite a famous figure. I knew better than to point either of those facts out. He was just trying to have a good time. I smirked at the thought of that woman going on and on about how good looking he was—little did she know he was sitting next to her!

Leaving his chalet, I tried not to notice that his heated floors melted some snow right off my boots. Surely, he was used to that. Priscilla and I were back outside, where I took the deepest breath of fresh air that I could muster while I processed what had just happened.

The key slid into the lock as it should have and turned easily. I let out the breath I was holding. It was going to be okay. I put Priscilla down in her warm bed while I tiptoed back out to my front door and grabbed the firewood I collected, not letting the door shut behind me. Bringing it back inside, the chill in the air tickled my throat.

"It sure got cold in here fast," I said to Priscilla, who was sitting on top of her blankets as she shivered dramatically, watching me load the wood stove. After it was full of wood, I took a long match from the coffee table that was sitting next to a candle and swiped it on its box. The zip of the flame was comforting and reassuring, but when I threw it into the stove, nothing happened. Watching the little flame move down the length of the match until it fizzled out—hmm—this *starting a fire* thing was harder than I thought.

"Priscilla, I knew I should have put you into Girl Scouts last summer," I said sarcastically, as I looked for some kind of paper I could throw inside to start the fire. Then it dawned on me: I had piles, if not *dozens* of manuscripts in the back of my car. Surely, in an emergency type of situation like this, burning one or three would be warranted? Heck, it wasn't like I didn't print them out on my own printer; I had them all still backed up on my computer. But the guilt of burning a book—be it in any form—rocked me. I worked out an elaborate plan in my head as I propped the door open and walked to my car to retrieve them: I would write down all of the important facts—author's name, title, and contact information—and the first thing I'd do when I returned to work was reprint them.

"*The Love Bear Goes to Space* by Terry Salmon." I read the first title aloud as I shoved it into the stove. "What does this book have to do with Jesus?" I asked, rhetorically, holding back a laugh. "I'm sorry, love bear. Your sacrifice is for central heating." I retrieved another match, zipped its strip, and waited for the inferno. Within seconds, I saw flames. The warmth quickly spread, but before I knew it, so did thick, black smoke. "What in the world, *Love Bear?*" The chalet was filling up with black smoke from the wood stove. I closed the door of the stove, locking its latch, but it just kept spreading. Jumping into action, I grabbed Priscilla, covered her head in my jacket, and ran to open a window. The only problem? The smoke was filling the room faster than I could move. We had no choice but to open the front door and stand outside while it cleared.

"I'm sorry, sweet girl." I kissed Priscilla on the head as her body trembled in the plunging temps, despite her wearing a jacket, boots and being zipped up cozy in my own jacket. After a few minutes of holding the door open, I heard a voice behind me.

"Is everything okay in there?" It was such a handsome, rugged, *cowboy* voice—I knew it could only be one person. Turning, I found myself face to face with Ford, who was wearing a black winter jacket, jeans, and what could only be described as "work boots." He had a baseball cap yanked halfway down his eyebrows, as if he was trying to conceal his identity again. But there was no concealing that jawline.

"No, not really," I sighed, knowing I was moving back into the territory of being a pain in someone's rear, but I didn't care. I was freezing, Priscilla was freezing. I peered over to the Sage Mountain Resort. "I think this trip is doomed. I should just go get a hotel room," I shrugged.

"What's wrong in there? Despite the power being out," Ford asked.

"The wood stove is spreading smoke everywhere, and I thought I'd, uh, air it out." His eyes widened as he ran inside, his forearm covering his mouth and nose. After a few minutes, he came back out to the porch.

"The chimney isn't working properly. Seems someone cut a few corners upon install." He squeezed the bridge of his nose with his fingers. "The chimney cap has to be higher than the ridge of the house. I can't believe this passed inspection." His annoyance went beyond neighborly. "You can't stay there unless the power comes back on." I nodded, thinking about my options and remembering the cute boutique hotel I walked past this morning on my way to the gondola. What was it—the *Tucked Inn,* perhaps?

"Okay. Hopefully the property managers can refund me for this. I spent a small fortune to stay here this week." I let myself commiserate for a moment.

"They will." Ford crossed his arms. I tilted my head, wanting to ask him how he knew that. Was he friends with them? Maybe he knew the owners? My mind went back to him having a key. Maybe he helped out. Like a superintendent situation. But why would the multi-millionaire face of skijoring need to be doing that?

"Thanks for your help, Ford. I just need to grab my bags. Would you mind, uh, holding Priscilla for a moment? I would hate for her to breathe in the smoke." His eyes widened again as I handed him my little bundle of joy. He didn't wrap her in his jacket like I had, so I knew I had to be fast.

Upstairs, I tossed everything I brought back into my suitcase and hastily zipped it shut. My ski boots went into a duffle. I brought those to the front porch and made one more quick trip back to the kitchen, where I put all of my food into a large reusable bag. *I hope I get a room with a fridge for this stuff,* I thought to myself. Back outside, Ford was picking up my luggage and loading it into the back of my Yukon.

"Thank you for your help. I really appreciate it." I reached out to take Priscilla from his arms but paused when I noticed she wasn't even shaking. He nodded, handing her over, and she immediately started the cold act again.

"You're welcome to come inside and warm up for a few minutes while you look for a room. I have a computer you can use." That didn't sound like such a bad idea. Going from hotel to hotel seemed daunting.

"I'd appreciate that. Thanks." Ford nodded and went ahead of me to open the door of his chalet, motioning for me to go inside first. It was like walking into a warm cloud. I stepped out of my shoes to be polite, sitting on his small entryway bench to do so. I also removed Priscilla's boots and thought I heard a chuckle coming from Ford when I did so.

Taking off her shoes was all Priscilla lived for at this moment: She immediately started *zooming* around his home and jumping on and off his couch in the process.

"I'm sorry—she's excited to be here, I think." I couldn't believe her burst of energy, but at the same time, I thought it was adorable. I peered over at Ford who didn't seem to react at all.

"That's fine by me. She needs to get her exercise somehow." He poured himself a cup of coffee, pointing to it. "Do you want one?"

I shook my head. "Better not, or I'll be up all night." He nodded and went into another room where I heard a computer boot up.

"It's all ready for you. I have the Sage Mountain Resort site pulled up for you. It has every single lodging option we have."

"Great. Thanks, Ford. I'll just be right back, Priscilla," I called out to her as it looked like she was a pinball bouncing around his furniture.

Inside of Ford's office, there was a beautiful floor to ceiling window that overlooked the horse stables across the way. The cold air was heavy and settled around the mountains, creating a dreamlike fog atmosphere.

His hand-carved wooden desk had a supple leather topper, attached with brass tacks. It was very western and as I looked around, I noticed all of it was. In the chalet I rented, everything was exquisitely modern and *alpine chic.* In Ford's chalet, it was like stepping into a ranch house. I liked it.

Adding in the dates of my nearly week-long stay, minus one night, yielded no results. "Okay, maybe I need to stay a few places." I took off half of the nights and looked for something the next three days. *Nothing.* "How about two nights?" I asked the computer as my searches became frantic. *Sorry, no results!* "Tonight. That gives me one night to pray for the roads to open and at least then, I could go back home!" *Sold out.*

Tiptoeing back to the living room, I tried to hide my expression from Ford, but it didn't work. He caught my eyes with his.

"Well?" he asked. I shook my head.

"Everything is. . . sold out." I swallowed the lump in my throat. "But it's okay. We have enough warm blankets, and surely the chalet won't be that bad without heat, and if the roads open back up. . ." Ford looked away, and I trailed off, recalling before the wood stove incident I could see my breath. It was bone chilling inside.

"You can stay here." He didn't make eye contact with me, but instead, walked to the window. The snow was falling again, hard. While it made for perfect conditions on the slopes, it was more than a little daunting to be trapped by it. In a town I wasn't from. In a stranger's chalet. A stranger that was in fact extremely gorgeous, which made it even more upsetting. Now, this handsome man was saying I could stay here? I looked around and saw that Priscilla was snoring loudly as she slept on a couch cushion. There was also a blanket half pulled up around her, which I didn't know if she burrowed under or. . .

"Where would I sleep?" All of his furniture was luxurious. His tooled leather couch didn't necessarily look like it was meant for a sleepover, and I certainly wouldn't be sharing his room. The idea of it got me so fired up, I felt angry. Is THAT his motivation here? Get me in his bedroom? Because it ain't happenin,' buddy. I'd rather camp in a frozen house than entertain that idea for even a second.

"In the guest bedroom. This has more than one room, you know." The relief washed over me, but the reality of sharing a home with a man who was not my husband sharpened my mind. The fact was, I had nowhere to go right now. There was a bedroom here that I would be welcomed to sleep in. I just had to keep my wits about me.

"I don't know, Ford. To be honest, I am feeling hesitant to cohabitate with a man who is not my husband." The words came out of my mouth faster than I could stop them. Here we go—the crazy train had left the station. This was usually where a man piped up to say I was "ridiculous" or "unbearable" to be around. I wanted to watch his expression, but he still faced the window.

"Are you married?" Ford asked, turning to me.

"No. I am just. . . Waiting for that, is what I mean." *Cringe.* Now, he probably had no idea what we were talking about. After a motionless moment, he nodded.

"I promise to be a gentleman, and we will get you back into your chalet as soon as possible. I'll send an email to the maintenance crew today."

"Thank you." Okay, this was fine. I just needed to keep those wits. And my dignity. And whatever I did, I did not need to fall for this gorgeous, introspective, quiet, brooding cowboy. *Lord, please put a barrier between me and this man so I don't form any ridiculous feelings for him.*

Ford showed me the room I would be staying in. It was downstairs, and I was relieved it had a lock on the door. There was one large picture window above the dresser, situated to watch the snow fall while lying in the down feather-filled bed. Ford's chalet was larger than the one I rented, to allow for this bedroom and his office plus another room turned into a gym. In my rented chalet, there were just the two rooms and the upstairs loft. It was dreamy and serene with its alpine style, and now, I was living in a cowboy world.

The pictures on the wall were western paintings of horses and snowy landscapes. There was almost nothing personal in this room, except for maybe one small, yellow feather on the counter. I picked it up—I couldn't help myself—when Ford came barreling in with my suitcases.

"I went out and got these." He set them down after carrying them effortlessly, as I still held the feather up in between us.

"This is. . . pretty." I couldn't have said anything lamer, I decided, and set the feather down.

"My cleaning crew found that. They thought this room needed some color." He shrugged and *almost* cracked a smile. Looking around, the furniture was dark wood, the bedding was crisp white, and the paintings were of light, colorless aesthetic. The feather was doing a lot of heavy lifting here, being the only pop in this room.

"This room *is* different from your other rooms," I said, trying to not be too inquisitive. Pushy. *Annoying.* But I couldn't help but notice just *how* out of the ordinary this room was compared to the rest of his chalet that was decked out in barnwood, leather, and *ski cowboy* aesthetic.

"Yeah, I've never used this room or had guests here. Until now."

"How long have you lived here?" I felt the questions bubbling up inside of me as I started with a simple one.

"A year." He ran his fingers through his beautiful, thick, brown hair. "Geez. Time really flies."

"No friends or family have come to visit you in that time frame?" I resisted crossing my arms as best as I could, but unless he was a friendless orphan, I started to feel defensive of this situation.

"Nah. My parents have passed away. I have a brother up on our family ranch in Big Horn, Wyoming, where I grew up, but we aren't close. And all of my friends have chalets of their own, or. . ."

"Or, what?" That was it. You can't make words spoken unsaid, and my pain-in-the-rear ways had come roaring back.

"We've gone our separate ways." Ford looked uncomfortable by my questions, or maybe the room felt that way. There was a tension here, but unlike the other men I'd dealt with over the years, I couldn't tell if Ford was annoyed with me like they had been. I didn't sense an aggravation behind his eyes. But maybe, something else. I couldn't put my finger on it. For now, I would let it go.

"Got it. Well, I'm honored to be your first guest. I hope we can get through to the property management company and get this resolved quickly."

"Unfortunately, I don't think they are going to be able to fix that chimney. I'm appalled that I didn't see it before today. That chalet was the last one to be finished and the only one I didn't personally inspect. Figures." Ford walked out of the guest bedroom and went and sat on the couch. I followed.

"Why would you personally inspect the chalets?" I lifted my brows at him. It took all the strength I had to resist tapping my foot while waiting for an answer.

"Because. . . I own them." My jaw dropped. He looked away, surely contemplating a way to climb up the power poles and restore power on his own. Where's a key and a kite when you need one?

"Well, that's nice. It's good to be diversified. Surely, an athlete can't compete forever." *Diversified?* What was I, a financial advisor? And my comment about his inevitable retirement was so, so *cringe.* I was about to duct tape my own mouth shut when he got up and walked to the window.

"Ain't that the truth."

Priscilla let out a loud snore and woke herself up. I went to her while she got refamiliarized with her surroundings.

"Did you take a good nappy?" I loved talking to her in baby talk, and she loved being treated like the little *princess* that she was. This time, however, she looked right past me, like it wasn't me that she was looking for. She sat up, turned, and locked her eyes on the back of Ford. Looked like my girl had a little crush on someone. "Should we go outside and go potty?" I knew if I didn't take her out every few hours, she would wake me up in the middle of the night to go out. And the last thing I wanted to do was to be traipsing around this chalet past midnight.

After getting her bundled up in a bright blue jacket, which was a little heavier than her pink one, and putting her snow booties back on, we headed for the door. Ford, still standing at the window watching the snow fall, walked over and opened the door for us.

"Thank you," I said, acknowledging his gentlemanly ways. Priscilla's eyes were still glued to him, and she even tried to sniff him as he stepped by us to get the door. He flipped a switch before shutting the door behind us, and the whole valley was lit up by his flood lights. It wasn't yet pitch black out, but the light had been so dim, it was hard to see. Now, I could see everything.

Priscilla's Inner Monologue

These boots might look fabulous on me, darling, but they are a far cry from Chanel.

Big, fat snowflakes were falling fast. I closed my eyes and stuck my tongue out to catch them, bringing waves of fond memories of my childhood back to me. After Priscilla was finished, we ran back to the door, frozen solid. Just thirty seconds being outside and my teeth were chattering, and I was covered in snow.

CHAPTER 4: FORD

SNOWBOUND HOSPITALITY

The storm weighed heavily on the rooftops. Plows were groaning in the distance and while the power outage was straining on the community, I was surprised that not more of the chalet guests had come knocking.

It was strange having guests. As I watched Presley and her little fluffy dog that was more bundled up than I'd ever seen any creature on earth navigate the outdoors in the snow, it made me feel something I hadn't experienced in a long time. Next thing you know that dog was going to have a set of spurs on those boots. I didn't know what it was. Annoyance? Acceptance? What I did know: this woman was *trouble*.

Presley sure did have a lot of questions. And I sure hated questions. It was making me remember why I was so relieved to break my phone earlier. That reminded me; I needed to get them into another chalet. I instinctively reached for my phone, and remembered again that it was shattered, so I looked at my watch. It was past five on a Friday; there was no one at the office tonight. With the roads shut down, what kind of crew was I really going to be able to get in here to fix that chimney? It was unlikely that it was going to get done in the short time this woman was here. Besides, I'd be out most of the week and the weekend with the Winter Games and all. I bet I'd barely see this woman. We'd be like two ships passing in the night. Well, three ships, if you counted Priscilla.

I didn't know what was more ridiculous—little dogs or their required *clothing.* Presley and her dog came racing back in the chalet and the dog waited patiently while Presley took off those little snow boots. The dog even stuck her legs out, one by one, as if to assist. There ain't nothing natural about a dog needing clothes or shoes.

Then she made an announcement about making a late dinner and asked if I wanted anything. Truthfully, I was starved after my day on the slopes, but I wasn't yet prepared to share a meal with this woman.

"I'm alright. I'll probably throw something on the stove in a minute." That did the trick, and she got to making her meal while her little dog, now wearing footed pajamas with pink snowflakes all over, sat on top of a pair of shoes I had on the floor and watched me. I tilted my head to the side and her eyes followed. Tilting it to the other side, she followed again. I didn't know if that meant she liked me or she hated me, but I decided she was just being protective of her mom. It was sort of funny, in a way, how much personality she had.

As Presley cooked, the aromas of her meal wafted right into my nostrils. She hummed a familiar tune while she stirred the pot with my wooden spoon. I wanted to ask her what song, as I couldn't necessarily *Shazam* it, but I just listened instead.

When I closed my eyes, it was almost like having Poppy back here with me. My dog, a much larger, respectable sized dog would be kind of where Priscilla was sitting. But he would be enjoying his chew bone instead of singling me out with an intense, obsessive gaze. It pained me to think of him; I missed that dog. My mind went back to the wedding photo I saw of Poppy; all of my old friends were probably at that wedding. Heck, *my* dog was probably the ring bearer. *Traitors.* Other than my brother, whom I was not close with, I was completely alone in the world. If only I could have ended the estrangement I had with God...

"Dinner's ready." Presley interrupted my thoughts. I opened my eyes and saw that she had two bowls of food on the table. "Nothing fancy—just some curry. I added a few things to it to jazz it up. I hope you don't have any food allergies." I looked at her like she was from another planet.

"I said I didn't want food?" I stood, not sure what I was supposed to do. She didn't back down.

"And it's the least I could do, since you are putting me and Priscilla up for the time being. So here, please eat the food I prepared." Taking a few cautious steps forward, the aroma of the food made my mind relent. It smelled delicious, and my stomach did a churn to let me know I was in fact starving. As I sat down on the opposite chair Presley was in, I reached for the utensils, when Presley put her palms together, closed her eyes, and started to pray—*out loud.*

"Lord, thank You for this meal. May it provide nourishment to our bodies. Thank You for this storm bringing lots of wonderful snow to Sage Mountain. Thank You for keeping Priscilla and me safe by bringing us to Ford. And we thank You for Ford. Without his hospitality, I don't know where we would be tonight. Please, Lord, bless him. In Your name, Amen." When her prayer was done—though I had been following along with her words—I had been watching her the whole time. The shine of her nail polish reflected under the light of my antler chandelier while her hands were pressed together. They were pressed together, because she was praying. My mind did some tumbling while I worked this out.

"Amen," I mumbled, realizing I was in the presence of a godly woman. I didn't come across those too often in my life these days. I guess you could've said because of my dating decision, I didn't come across any women anymore. I took a bite of the curry. The chances of it *not* being delicious were slim to none, and I was right. It was fantastic. It was nice to have something different. My meals mainly consisted of "red meat and potatoes," and I didn't detect either in this dish.

Presley didn't say much while we ate, which was fine with me. She was guarded, but I was, too. It was a relief knowing that we both had our walls up, and this wasn't going to turn into something awkward. As I took the last bite of the red curry, a squeaking noise came from under the table.

Her dog, Priscilla, had a toy in her mouth that she was squeaking ever so softly, as if to get my attention. Presley looked under the table, asking the dog to hand her the toy so she could throw it, appearing to appeal to this dog's every whim and fancy. But, the dog didn't budge, keeping her eyes on me.

"I believe she may want *you* to throw it." Presley put her hands up with an apologetic look on her face, as if the simple task of throwing a dog toy would put me over the edge, and I'd send them out in the cold. Before I could, she reached under the table and picked the dog up, who still held the toy securely in her bite.

While she held Priscilla in one arm, she picked up her dish with the other, quietly loading the dirty items into my dishwasher. I stayed at the table, considering if I wanted to throw the dog's toy for her or not. I decided that if it happened again, I would throw it for her.

I retreated to my bedroom after Presley and her pooch went to the guest bedroom and called out goodnight. I replied with a simple "night" and put my bowl into the dishwasher and turned it on. Tomorrow, I had a long training day—the last one before the Games—with my teammate, Chase, my horseback rider, so I prepped some oatmeal that would cure in the fridge overnight. Normally, I'd make a big breakfast, but now that I had guests, I was aware they might have a different sleeping pattern than I did. I was an up at dawn sort of man; I remembered how much that irritated Poppy. She would always go on about her needing her beauty sleep. Yes, we were crazy incompatible, but I cringed as I thought about the patterns we had set. We shouldn't have known that about each other, because we weren't married. While we didn't live together, I had made so many mistakes in my life that I didn't see a reason to improve upon it or set new standards when I met her. I wanted her to fit perfectly into my life that I was creating, as it grew further and further from God.

Closing the door of my bedroom, I found myself tiptoeing around the room. Holding the light switches tightly to ensure no sounds were made. For all I knew, Presley was up reading or a deep sleeper, but I did it anyway.

Crawling into bed, I reflected upon the changes today brought. Presley's prayer was at the top of my mind. There were so many areas of my life that were tarnished—my relationship with God being just one of the many—but her prayer seemed so *easy*. Was it just that easy to come back to Him? For my transgressions to be forgiven, for God to forget them forever? I wondered.

Life without my phone meant no alarm set. The moment I opened my eyes the next morning, I sat up in a panic, thinking

I'd already missed my training session at 8. Opening my automatic blinds, the light for this time of year looked like it could be anywhere from 6:30–7:30. Scrambling to my closet, I threw on some clothes that I would wear under my ski things in case I had slept in. Opening the door, I stopped in my tracks at the aroma and sizzling that only bacon could make.

"Good morning. I hope I didn't wake you." Presley, in her ski clothes and hair pulled back into a braid, looked at me with her clean face and bright blue eyes. Her dog ambled quickly over to my feet, standing up on her hind legs as if to crawl up mine.

"No, you didn't. What time is it?" I looked around as if I had forgotten that I didn't have a clock in sight. I really did rely on my cell phone for everything these days, and I hated that.

"A quarter to seven. I had to check the time on your computer; I hope you don't mind. I can't seem to find my phone charger anywhere. Roads closed, powers out, and not a cell phone between us." She looked back up at me. "Do you have somewhere you need to be?" Her inquisitive look from yesterday returned.

"I have to be at the track at 8 sharp for my last training session. Games are this weekend, after all." She nodded, turning the bacon in the pan. There was at least a pound of bacon being fried, and I found myself hoping that some of that was for me.

"Want some of this? I couldn't find any Tupperware here to save it in the fridge, so I just made the whole package." I smirked at the thought of her looking through my cabinets to find Tupperware. I was sure she was extremely disappointed to see that I barely had the serving ware for two. Though I had a company that helped furnish this home, I didn't see a need for an extravagant number of *things.* Nope, nothing extra. Just the essentials.

"Sure," I said nonchalantly, but was thrilled. The oatmeal I made last night would still serve me as an extra kick on my way to the track, but this protein would help me out better. The toaster popped, revealing two slices of thick and crusty sourdough bread: *my favorite.* I watched as Presley sliced an heirloom tomato up, topping each piece of bread and following it with the bacon.

"Just give me two minutes for the eggs." I watched as she cracked colorful farm eggs over the cast iron skillet, expertly flipping them each after a moment. They popped and sizzled as I made a fresh brew of pour-over coffee.

"Would you like a cup?" My offer was slight in comparison to the feast she was preparing. She nodded.

"Sure. I like mine with heavy cream. I have some in your fridge." She smiled, beaming her bright white teeth. I opened the fridge and found it full of colorful vegetables and all sorts of extravagant items. The cream was sitting on the top shelf; it was from a small, local farm and the label read "Organic" and "Certified Humanely Treated." Having grown up on a Wyoming ranch myself, I like that she shopped locally and cared about the origins of her food. What was I doing? Admiring the food this stranger in my home shopped for? *Ford, get your head in the game.*

After pouring her coffee, I set her mug and the creamer on the table. She plated the food, topping the delicious-looking toasts with the fried eggs. Instead of having mine at the table, I graciously accepted the plate, and I ate it standing up, hovering over the sink. Her eyes darted to the table and if I could hear her thoughts, I'd bank on her wondering why I wasn't going to sit down. But despite having plenty of time this morning, I also had plenty of reservations about this situation, this woman, and now, this little dog who was looking up at me intently while I ate, hoping I'd drop a bite.

As I looked down at the furry creature, who today was wearing a blue sweater with a matching bow on her head-around a little ponytail at that, I couldn't help but notice she was getting impatient. It seemed the little *princess* was used to getting table scraps and treats. I didn't know which of these foods were safe, so when my last bite consisted of a small leftover piece of bread, half the size of my thumb, I let it drop. She caught it in her mouth like the little hunter-gatherer that she was inside under all the clothes. The boots. The hairdo.

Dogs were meant to be wild. I had always taken this into account when I raised them and with my last dog. . . before Poppy took him with her. He was still not a looming giant, but Australian Shepherds are a respectable size. Let's just say he could fend for himself if he got outside unsupervised for a moment. This little creature, on the other hand; I didn't think she could survive at a pet store without help.

Once she devoured the bite of bread, she gave me a little wag. I took it as her way of thanking me. She immediately went to my pair of boots that were sitting by the front door and sat on them, toppling them over in the process.

As I put my plate in the dishwasher and thanked Presley for preparing it, I walked over to her dog, who was holding onto my boots for ransom. She was probably going to require another piece of bread.

"What's going on here?" I whispered to her, putting my hands on my waist. I had to admit her personality was entertaining. Presley jumped up into action, once again, as if her dog was going to get them thrown out into the cold.

"Oh, Priscilla. Come here, sweetie. He needs those boots." She scooped up her dog and went back to the table where she was cleaning up the leftover crumbs. As I sat on the bench to put on my boots, I found myself having a hard time mentally preparing for the day with them around.

"Have a great training day," Presley said, as she finished wiping down the counters after cooking. She really was trying to be a good guest.

"Thanks. And thank you for, uh, cleaning up." Presley nodded. My words were weak, as if my coffee never hit my bloodstream. I considered having one more cup before I left, as I knew I still had time to do so, but something was telling me to leave. Get away from the chalet. Away from this woman.

I walked outside without another word. Out in the cold, I realized I forgot my gloves. What a ridiculous mistake. I looked at my hands. I had always had thick skin—literally, not figuratively, much to my own chagrin—and I had trained before without gloves. But this close to the games, risking tearing up my hands on a rough rope? That would be a really stupid thing to do. Ugh, was I really considering going without GLOVES so that I could avoid more time with my house guest? What was happening to me?

Turning back to the door of my own home, I paused. *Should I knock?* Then, it dawned on me: This woman didn't have a key *or* the code to my chalet. If she got back before I did—which was very likely, as training could turn into an all-day affair once I got into caring for my animals—she would be out in the cold once again. The door opened while I contemplated life's biggest questions, and Presley was surprised to see me on the porch. She was wearing her ski helmet, goggles on top, and had her ski boots on. Her skis must have still been outside of her chalet next door.

"What's up?" she asked, her eyebrows closing in on each other with her squint. The snow was gently falling around us, and the dull light made it hard to see.

"I forgot to give you the door code." Presley looked relieved.

"Oh, of course. Thank you," she said, and looked at me expectantly.

"Yep." I stood there, thinking about how my gloves were just on the other side of the door. Along with that cup of coffee, my oatmeal that I was going to have for a snack, and her little dog that I felt could see right through the facade that was me holding this all together.

"Well? What is it?" Presley couldn't hide her impatience, but she did a great job trying.

"Oh, sorry. It's zero, three, zero, one." She repeated it a few times.

"Great. I got it memorized. What is that, your birthday or something?"

"Good guess," I nodded.

"Nice. That's coming up fast! Happy birthday." She playfully punched me in the shoulder.

"I'm not really into birthdays. Or holidays," I said, shrugging it off. Presley just nodded.

"Honestly, I feel the same way. They can be so hard. Especially when you're single." We stood in silence for a moment. "Well, have a great one! I want to catch the first chair." And she was off. She was mighty speedy, despite her clunky ski boots as she snatched up her skis, brushed the snow off of them, threw them over her shoulder, and disappeared into the busy street of skiers ahead.

Going back inside, I shut the door behind me and took a deep breath. The dog was excited to see me and acted like I'd been gone for hours as she hopped around me, wanting to be picked up. For a moment, I must have forgotten what I was doing or all of those walls I had tightly built around my heart because I fulfilled the wish of Presley's dog and scooped her up like a football. She excitedly panted, wriggling around in my arms, trying to climb up towards my face. I held her in the crook of my arm while I made the extra cup of coffee, pouring it into a traveler cup. I found my gloves and shoved them into my jacket pocket that hung near the door. Apparently, I had forgotten that, too. And lastly, I grabbed the oatmeal out of the fridge and gave the container a shake.

As I leaned to set the dog down, she let out what I would call a combination of a bark and a groan. It was like she was threatening me if I did so. I couldn't help but laugh.

"I gotta go, little girl." She stomped around in a circle before letting herself up on my couch. "You're pretty funny, you know that?" I reached for the blanket that lay over the side of the couch; Presley must have tidied up this morning. I laid it around Priscilla. I couldn't even think of her name with a straight face. I wasn't a silly guy, but once I found something funny, I couldn't ever go on again without laughing about it.

I left my chalet for the final time and got into my white Ram 3500 truck. First, I went to the stables and latched onto my horse trailer. I made sure the horses had plenty of hay, fresh water, and that the water heater to keep it from forming a giant block of ice was in proper working order. Thankfully, the stable had a generator, too.

Topping off the generator with diesel fuel, I brought Buckshot out to the trailer. "Here we go, boy. It's our last training day until the Winter Games." Buckshot was my strongest horse, but he was also the largest. He was at least two hands taller than Whiskey and Outlaw. One gallop from him could pull me farther than the others, but I also had to have more control for this reason. Knowing when to let up on the rope was crucial.

Once we got to the training track, the crews for the winter games were hard at work next door prepping the game track. We weren't allowed to do any practice runs on the official track, which led to some competitors having bouts of pre-game anxiety, but not me. This being my fifth time competing in the games—and the last—I knew that track like the back of my hand.

My rider, Chase Mentock, was waiting for me at the entrance.

"You know, normally in this situation, I would be bringing my own horse." Chase started off the morning with a jab.

"And if you had a horse, I would let you." I reached out and shook his hand. Chase was a great guy who was an expert horseman, but since moving to Sage Mountain to skijor with me full time, he had yet to find housing he could afford, let alone horses. As it was, he had a wife and a baby and did not need another mouth to feed. He worked full time as a horse trainer, which in this ski community wasn't exactly the biggest booming business, but he was making it work. His love of riding for skijorers helped fuel his decision for living here, and I was grateful and compensated him well when we won—we split the winnings right down the middle. Chase and I were a team.

As Chase saddled Buckshot, I slid into my ski boots and got my best slalom racer skis out of the back seat of my pickup and started waxing them. The conditions for the games were perfect: compacted snow with a powdery top layer hiding icy spots. The jumps at the training track had been built a touch higher than the actual track had done in the past, per my request, so my training would keep me sharp enough to handle whatever they could throw at me. The only things our training area was missing were the flamethrowers that would go off as skijorers passed certain points—an entertainment ploy, purely for the audience, but was it enough of a surprise that it could throw someone off? Sure.

"You ready?" Chase asked as he was sitting in the saddle on Buckshot. He was wearing his black cowboy hat, a pair of blue jeans, and a heavy felted coat. Then there was me, in full-blown ski gear, slipping on my helmet. I followed him over to the start of the track just a few paces away and clipped into my skis.

"Ready as I'll ever be," I said nodding. Taking the rope in my hand, I started thinking the same way I did at every race practice or with hundreds of spectators.

People had been hard on me my entire life. I was raised to be a ranch hand—labor for my parents. The only sport I could muster the time for was skijoring, since it took place in the winter when ranching was a little less intensive. Our cattle wintered in a lower pasture and the ranch next door fed them;

in exchange for the relief and hay, my parents gave them five head of cattle, along with a meager payment. Back then, it was a good business practice. That cattle were enough to start their own mega ranch, which they did, of premium bloodline angus.

My parents allowed my sport and graciously supported me with the funds to get skis and boots at the local Ski Swaps. But they never really understood me. They loved me, but they wanted me to follow in their footsteps and be a rancher. To pass on the legacy to me was everything. Thankfully, my older brother Clint was on board with that vision. He was ten years older than me and already growing into a man when I was born. He had great responsibilities and was eager to do them. Sure, I was a cowboy through and through; I just didn't want to raise cattle—to be confined to an idea that my entire world was going to be that same plot of land. I wanted adventure. To see the world.

I was there to work hard, which I certainly did. But the moment I had the chance to escape that life, I jumped ship into this one. My family never reached out to me much after that, which hurt me worse. My mother died a few years later, after a battle with an illness they didn't even disclose to me. Then, my dad went. Clint did call me right before that one, but I was on a short trip to Italy, and I couldn't exactly leave. That decision had haunted me. And now, as I navigated the jumps and corners of this racetrack, using the rope of the racing horse in front of me to slack as I sped up and tightened as I slowed, I couldn't help but feel regret.

I never considered that I wouldn't be married with a family of my own by now. A chance to do it differently. To right the wrongs of my own life. But after Poppy. . . and my fall from God, which, to be honest with myself, happened long before her—I made a decision that I wouldn't date until I was back with God. Forgiven. Washed clean from sin.

A swift movement around a corner and for a split second, I almost let go of the rope. Did I even want to do this sport? Did I enjoy it? I was here because I was good at it. Some said, "The best in the business." I had a wall full of trophies to prove it.

"Just one more race," I mumbled to myself as we finished our first time through the track. After the Winter Games 2026, the persona I'd so neatly crafted of Ford Prescott could fade out with the melting of the snow. I just didn't have a clue what I was going to do after that.

"That was our best time yet, Ford," Chase beamed, pulling a stopwatch out of his jacket. We were both panting as we caught our breath.

"Go again?" I asked, and he nodded.

CHAPTER 5: PRESLEY
POWDER FOR TWO

As hard as I tried not to think of him, with every turn of my skis and as every flake of snow touched the tip of my nose, I thought of Ford. *Keep your dignity, Presley. Do not fall for the brooding cowboy!* My self-talk did not sway my thoughts, however, and unlike yesterday, I was happy to see the hours fly by.

Come two in the afternoon, I decided to stop for a cup of hot cocoa. The chairlift brought me to a scenic diner at the top of the mountain called *Ellie's.* It was a cozy diner that smelled like cinnamon and espresso. They served every flavor of coffee and hot chocolate under the sun, and had a line out the door. Thankfully, there were menus hanging from about every angle so while I stood in line, I could mull over my options.

Did I want a salted caramel hot chocolate or a white raspberry? As the line inched closer, I saw they also had baked goods galore. Checking my fitness tracker, I'd burned countless calories today shredding up the slopes, so I decided I had earned an extra little something. Finally, it was my turn to order.

"May I have a salted caramel hot chocolate and an eggnog muffin?" Just ordering it aloud made my mouth water.

"Coming right up," the barista smiled. She had long, blonde hair in braids and a beanie that read, "Snow Bunny." A man came out from the kitchen and added a few more baked goods to the cooler. He was strikingly handsome, and I lost my train of thought when she gave me the total, signaling me to pay.

"Miss? I said it's $10.39." She smiled graciously, acting as if it wasn't out of the ordinary for him to make a woman's mind stop working. I quickly swiped my card and added a generous tip, pretending not to notice when he walked away. As she made my drink, I leaned over and asked her a question.

"What is it with the men here in Wyoming? Why are they all so. . . handsome? Do you bake them from scratch up here?" She giggled at my question.

"Don't I know it. It's their cowboy genes. Like, genetics I mean. Of course, it doesn't hurt how they look in a pair of *Levi's*, either." She motioned to the man standing in the kitchen, who could now be seen through the window on the door. "I would love to take him to church on Sunday. But he's a real quiet type. Can't tell if I'm driving him nuts, or he's going to one day decide that I'm the one for him." I nodded, knowing all too well how she felt. As she handed me my drink and a little paper bag containing my muffin, I walked over to a table and sat down to eat it. My ski boots were firmly planted in the ground. Normally, I liked to eat with one leg under the other, but this was forcing me to sit properly, and it was difficult to get comfortable, but I didn't have a hard time savoring the muffin. It was absolutely delicious.

A little flyer on the table caught my eye as I was savoring the flavors. "Baked goods are made in Maple Haven, Wyoming from The Pumpkin Perk Cafe. Shipped frozen and baked fresh in our lodge." *Maple Haven... Now, that sounds like a cute place.*

Well, that was the longest I'd gone without thinking of Ford that day. Turned out, all I needed was a constant stream of baked goods and sugar to keep my mind preoccupied. Getting up from the table, I took care of the garbage and headed back to the slopes.

Warm and energetic from the sugar rush, I decided to go on a more challenging run. Usually, I stuck to the intermediate groomers—the runs that the plows flatten out and don't have any hidden moguls that might have killed my knees.

I'd been doing those the last two days, though, and I was ready for something that kept up with this new, false sense of energy I had. And maybe it would keep my mind off of a certain someone.

I took a chairlift for a run called "Dill Pickle" that said it was a Black Diamond. Usually, those are for experts only, but according to the map, this one split off into three different blue runs, so I had adequate chances to abort the mission if need be.

On the ride up, I was sitting next to a couple who were gently arguing. "I don't feel safe going down this slope, Jerry. Why don't I just ride the chairlift back down and meet you in the middle?" she said, to which he replied, "You can't ride the chairlift back down, dear. Only gondolas can be ridden both ways at Sage Mountain." Then, she started to panic, as this one led to only Black Diamonds. I knew the feeling, having been very scared the first few expert runs I did years ago.

"I'm sorry to interrupt," I said quietly, "but this run doesn't look that bad. If you'd like, I can go first and scope out the easiest route for you to take." She nodded.

"I would love that, thank you, because Jerry here is too good of a skier to remember what an easy route looks like," she giggled, and I could feel the energy between them change.

"Great. Don't worry; even on the hardest mountains, there's always an easier way down." I didn't know where the words came from but for today, it felt like God. As we rode the rest of the way in silence, I thought of the hard mountain I had been on this last year. That I had put myself on. I was self-isolating with workloads that were not sustainable. I had made huge life changes to stop seeking out dates and while that brought me peace, it also made me feel incredibly lonely. And, I hadn't taken any extra time for myself to reflect upon these things. Yet, here I was on a vacation to work out these thoughts, and I found myself *shacked up* with my gorgeous cowboy neighbor. *God, You really do have a sense of humor.*

After the chair dropped us off at the top, I saw the way down that was the easiest, but still a great challenge. I told her to follow my tracks, to which she did confidently. Her partner, Jerry, stayed by her side in solidarity.

This Black Diamond was known for its steepness. I had to take a few breaks on the way down for how hard I was working to not fall forward, but the challenge to my muscles and skiing ability was welcomed. I enjoyed every moment of it, even when it felt unbearably hard. "Thank you, Lord, for skiing!" I shouted, as I tore through the powdery snow. He had blessed this mountain with an amazing amount of fresh moisture—so much that it knocked out the power of my chalet. Again, I laughed at the circumstances.

As we all made it down to the first fork in the run, they had several options of easy diversions, including a long green cat track that circled around the whole mountain. It might have taken an extra hour to get down, but if you really needed to use it, you could have.

"Hey, thank you. It was nice skiing with you. You're a really good skier," the woman who held her hand out to shake mine said. "It's Stella, by the way."

"Nice to meet you, Stella. I'm Presley." Jerry put his arm around his lady.

"Are you here visiting, or do you live here? I'm always looking for ladies to ski with. The local women's skiing group didn't gather this year, and it's really put a damper on my progress."

"I wish I lived here! I'm just up from Denver for the week."

"Oh, you're here for the Winter Games? This place should be a mad house right now, but the highway shut down. We totally lucked out with all of this fresh pow to ourselves!"

"I haven't thought much about the Winter Games. Didn't even realize that I came on the same week as that," I grinned, not wanting to offend a local regarding my lack of knowledge for their largest event of the year.

"Yeah, Jerry here is a huge fan of Theo McCain. The ski jumper." I nodded in recollection of the name.

"Isn't he hosting the Games?" I think I heard that on the radio.

"Yep. And Jerry is taking his *Wheaties* poster for him to sign. What a dork!" Stella playfully punched him in the shoulder and giggled. "Well, maybe I'll see you around! Have a great rest of your stay here in Sage Mountain." We said our goodbyes, and I watched them ski away, opting for a blue groomer called *Bigfoot.*

My legs were tired and despite my afternoon sugary treat, my stomach was starting to growl. The chairlifts and gondolas in the distance started showing less people—last chair was coming up quick. Instead of fighting to get one more run, I opted to ski down all the way to the bottom of this one instead.

Skiing was usually a lot of time spent in prayer for me. I prayed for my safety, my clarity, my choices, and for those around me. I prayed in thanks for the fun experience. I loved being outdoors, and it was times like these that I realized how prohibitive my career was of that. The creative thoughts started flowing to me in the ways that I'd like to improve my life when I returned to Denver. Maybe I'd find an open-air office that I could work out of? No, that wouldn't work. Half the year, it was too cold. Maybe I'd take on less work? I liked the sound of that one.

As I contemplated what I could do to have more of God's beautiful creation surrounding my everyday life when I returned home, my thoughts went back to Ford. How would he and I end this arrangement? Would we exchange phone numbers? Or would this just be one of those wild stories that I told ten years from now about the week I spent in the chalet next door?

I was reminded that the power could come back on at any minute. Wasn't that a good thing, though? It would probably have been for the best. Before Ford got sick of me. Before he thought I was too talkative. Too inquisitive. *Too much.*

A pit formed in my stomach as I considered what would happen if he thought these things. And even if he didn't, I'd been so hurt by men I'd dated in the past—men who barely knew me at all, but didn't hold back their harsh judgments of me because they felt threatened or put off by me. It changed the mechanics of how I acted around people. I no longer felt the freedom to be myself.

As I made each turn, I considered in my head what God thought of this fear. I was a person with so much love to give. Why was I hiding behind past hurts and judgments? I always treated people with respect and kindness. Why didn't I instead lead with this love and God's grace?

Starting today—no, right that moment—I was no longer going to tiptoe around people in my life in fear that they might not like who I was. Ford included.

Reaching the bottom of the slopes, I kicked off my skis when I ran out of skiable terrain and put them over my shoulder. My clunky ski boots had me walking robotically on the paved sidewalks that I realized now were heated. This was an expensive place, Sage Mountain. A lot of development had happened here just in the last few years since the private airport was put in. A fleeting thought crossed my mind: Could I ever afford to live in a place like this? Excitement rushed through my veins as I contemplated it. It wasn't that I didn't like Denver, but my workload was crushing my soul, and I didn't exactly have a place that I could just ski out of when winter called. I was imagining what mountain biking was like here in the summer, as

I'd heard they converted the ski runs into trails for bikes when I made it back to the chalet. *Ford's chalet.*

Out of respect, I gave the door a gentle knock before entering the keypad. For all I knew, he could have been walking around without a shirt on and not expecting me. My cheeks went hot at the thought of it. *Pull yourself together, Presley!*

"Hello, Presley," Ford called out to me, as I entered the chalet. He was fully dressed, thankfully, but his position on the couch with Priscilla on his lap was still bringing all the feels. The self-talk wasn't enough. I needed prayer, and I needed it as soon as possible.

"Hey," I replied back, delayed. "How are you?" I sat on the bench of his entry way mud room and began unbuckling my ski boots.

"I'm tired," he said, with not a spark to be heard in his voice. He looked exhausted. Priscilla, on the other hand, looked absolutely full of it.

"I better take her out really quick," I said, as I took my first steps out of my ski boots. If my feet could scream from relief, they would. It felt so good to be out of them.

"She already went out. I got here about twenty minutes ago and took her out. On her leash. I couldn't figure out the boots, though." He looked at me for approval. I nodded, considering her paws must be absolutely frozen. They could get blistered from the cold—split and hurt. I hurled towards her, hesitating. But she looked fine. She was wagging her tail, happy to see me, though she wasn't moving. Priscilla wanted to be with Ford. It took everything I had, but I patted her on the head and stepped back.

"Thank you for taking her out, Ford," I smiled, releasing my breath. I remembered the promise I had just made myself not long ago on the slopes about being my true self that God created. So, here we go. "What's for dinner?" Ford had a confused look on his face for a moment, surprised by my question.

"Oh, uh, I don't know. What would you like?" I laughed at his response.

"I'm just teasing. I have all the food I need, and I'm more than happy to prepare something for the both of us again. I really enjoy cooking for others," I said. He smiled, quite possibly for the first time since I'd known him.

"Okay," he said, the words softly leaving his mouth.

I hung up my ski jacket on his coat rack and walked to the kitchen, then analyzed what I could put together for dinner for two. If I used what I brought, and some tortillas from his pantry and cheese from his fridge, I could just about make chicken enchiladas.

"Ford?" I hollered, my voice carrying across the chalet to him in the living room. The open concept chalet didn't *really* warrant my hollering like that, but I felt *excited* to be sharing a meal with someone and like Priscilla, I just felt happy. Full of it. And I felt freedom from worrying about how I was coming off while I led in what the Holy Spirit had empowered me with: an abundance of love. *Thank you, Lord.* After a moment, he didn't answer. I walked around the wall of the kitchen and saw that he had dozed off on the couch with Priscilla in his lap. She was looking at me with a look as if to say, "This one is mine." I smiled and shook my head.

Priscilla had always been a silly little dog. As I shredded the cheese for the enchiladas, I remembered how she acted towards my dad when they met. She started twirling like a ballerina. She's always liked men, which a friend told me was a great thing because some dogs are afraid of men. Ford was no different. Priscilla took an instant liking to him, and it was adorable. Hopefully when we get back into our chalet, she wouldn't miss him and start acting out.

Wrapping the shredded chicken into the tortillas with some red sauce and cheese, the oven preheated. Out of the corner of my eye, in the quickly dimming light of the outside, fat snowflakes started to fall again. The cold air was starting to frost around the windows. With my phone being off these last few days, I had felt freer than I had in years, but I was starting to wonder what was happening in the outside world. Was the highway still shut down? Was there more snow on the way?

As the enchiladas baked, I decided to dig through my bag for that pesky cell phone charger and reboot my phone for a few minutes to see what was happening. For all I knew, someone had been trying to get a hold of me. Likely, they had, but I was content being disconnected for the time being. I made a plan as I found my charger, that I wouldn't check my email. When I plugged my phone in, I decided I also wouldn't check my voicemail. I'd skim my texts and send my mom one that I was here and having a great time. Then, I'd check the weather and power off again.

Once it came back on, it sounded like a *Triple 7's* machine in Las Vegas with its dinging. *Be strong, Presley.* I blurred my eyes, pulling the phone out of focus as I tried to put on blinders to anything work related. There was a slew of texts from my assistant, Jenny, and the few words I skimmed while clearing the notifications said things like, "launch a success," and "hope you are having fun." I *was* having fun. And despite my not wanting to see the texts, seeing them brought a freeing feeling to my body.

I sent my mom a text about the beautiful location I was enjoying this week and checked the weather forecast. My jaw dropped.

"Weather forecasters say this storm is surpassing the totals they initially thought possible. Expect another 12–18 inches tonight, with more on the way. Looks like the 2026 Winter Games this weekend will be one for the books."

I looked out of my bedroom at Ford on the couch with his eyes still closed. He was completely still, and it looked like Priscilla had fallen asleep now, too. I hated to wake him, but this news was kind of important. Right?

"Ford," I whispered, trying to respectfully wake him. I put my hand on his shoulder to gently nudge him, and I was very intrigued at how muscular it felt. He opened his eyes slowly.

"Oh, I'm sorry, I must have fallen asleep on you." Ford rubbed his beautiful light green eyes. "I went really hard today."

"That's okay, and I'm so sorry to wake you, but I finally got my phone on and, well, look at this," I said, handing him the phone so he could read it for himself. A smile crossed his face.

"That's fantastic," he said, as my eyes widened in disbelief.

"It *is?* What if—well, what if the roads don't open back up and the spectators can't come? What if we get snowed in? What if all those things happen *AND* the power doesn't come back on, and I'm stuck here, with you?" I pleaded, pacing as I spoke. My mind was going rampant as I waited for his reply. He just shrugged.

"Things like this can always happen here in the mountains. That's why I have a generator. Less spectators means less distractions, and the camera crews came a few days ago as they are doing promos, so, the show will go on."

"And?" I hate that I did it, but I *gently* stomped my foot at the rest of my unanswered questions.

"And, I own all of the chalets. If you got stuck here for weeks on end, we have nine other options to put you up when someone checks out, which is inevitable that they will."

"How, when the roads are closed, will someone check out? Where will they go?" My mind was on overdrive. Part of me was spiraling into worry, while the other part was relieved that I had met the man who could at least host me while I was there.

"The private airport is open, as far as I know. I saw a jet leaving this morning. There's always a way out, Presley." Was this a secret metaphor for him wanting me to leave? I wondered. But, I didn't want to worry about how badly he wanted to get rid of me right now. This break was supposed to be relaxing and right now, I was acting crazy because I felt *crazy* anxious. I remembered my go to Bible verse about not worrying about anything and let the calm and peace of God wash over me.

"I'm sorry for overreacting. I can get a little. . . *High strung* sometimes."

"You're fine," Ford said, looking down at his lap as if noticing for the first time that Priscilla had made her bed on his legs. "Hi," he said, looking at her. She looked up at him and gave the tiniest little wag in reply. It melted my heart.

The oven chimed, letting us know that dinner was ready. I skated to the kitchen in my thick wooly socks and opened the door of the oven. The delicious smells wafted through the chalet, and it was divine.

"I hope you like chicken enchiladas," I hollered, not waiting for a reply before I started plating them. Enchiladas were best served while piping hot and when the cheese was melted to near-liquid form.

Ford walked over, Priscilla not an inch from his feet as she kept up with him. I put out her food bowl that I had prepared while I was cooking, and she excitedly went to it and started in. I left Ford's plate on the kitchen counter as he didn't choose to sit with me last time at the table, so I didn't want to smother him by forcing him to. But, I was elated when he picked it up and followed me to the table where he sat across from me. Immediately, I jumped into prayer.

"Lord, we thank You for this food that will bring nourishment to our tired bodies. I thank You for never leaving or forsaking me, though I do not deserve Your grace time after time. And for giving me the opportunity to meet Ford, who has been a perfect steward of charity to put us up. Please bless him, Lord, for his kindness. In Your name, Amen." I trailed off during prayer, but Ford's quiet "Amen" barely was audible. He paused for a moment and slowly started moving his fork.

"This is awesome. Thank you, Presley," Ford beamed, after taking a bite. "I can't remember the last time I had enchiladas."

"Well, there's more where that came from, then." I didn't know why I said that, but I rolled with it. "I mean, I love to cook."

"That's what you said." He smiled, but it almost looked forced. The man was exhausted.

"Yes. I love to cook, and I haven't been able to cook for someone else in years," I said, immediately contemplating if that made me sound *desperate.* Ugh, there I go again, worrying to death about what this man thought of me. *Lord, help me out. Ford's opinion of me does not matter. I just want to be kind and respectful.*

"I don't know that I like to cook, but I sure like to eat." Ford's serving was disappearing fast. I sipped the sparkling Italian soda I brought while he opted for water.

As we ate, and he got a heaping second serving, I noticed the sheer size of the table. Perfect for puzzling, and I just so happened to have brought a puzzle with me. Could you really take a ski trip in a sleepy snowy village without putting together a jigsaw? I didn't think so. I also noticed how quiet it was there. I felt a twinge of nostalgia and craved some music.

Pulling my phone out of my pocket, I opened my music app and scrolled until I found an aptly titled *après-ski* mix. The first song was soft and serene.

"You don't mind, do you?" I motioned to the phone that played music while we ate. He shook his head. The song ended short, and the second song to come up sounded like it was playing at a rave. "Oh my…" I trailed off, shutting down the app.

"If that's the kind of music you like, head down to the base of the ski resort. There's a DJ there five days a week blasting that," he smirked, as he finished his meal.

"No, I'm afraid not. I'm more into the oldies. Nothing from this century has won me over yet. I have a record collection at home. The way a record player fills a space with sound is just incredible. It might not be the crispest way to play a tune, but it sure feels the most… right." Ford smiled.

"You'll like this then." He got up and slid his chair back into the table, taking his dish to the sink. I got up to follow him as we went into his office. He revealed inside of a large built-in cabinet a record player and a small collection of records. "Go ahead and play something from here, if you'd like. I'm going to hit the shower." He left, heading upstairs to his room and shut the door behind him.

"Now we're talking!" I started thumbing through the collection and was pleasantly surprised that we had music tastes in common. I wasn't far into his cabinet when I realized the man had more Elvis albums than I was even aware existed. And I *loved* listening to Elvis. Kind of a chicken and the egg situation, considering my name and all, but I'd listened to him all of my life. So had my mother, who passed on her love for his tunes to me with my namesake. I swiftly put on one of his records and placed the needle at the beginning. As the delicious sound filled the room, I felt at home.

By the time Ford returned downstairs, I was halfway through the album and had 1,000 puzzle pieces scattered around half of his dining room table, on the side that we hadn't been eating at. The dishes were already in the dishwasher, and the counters had been wiped down. Priscilla was working on a *Kong* toy with a tablespoon of peanut butter inside as her prize. My hot tea was steeping a delicious peppermint scent, and I was having the time of my life. The song changed to a romantic slow crooner. I stood.

"Do you want to dance?" I asked Ford, who looked like I just asked him the secrets of the universe.

CHAPTER 6: FORD
TRACKS BACK TO GOD

I lied when I told her I was going to shower. Really, I had that urge to pray again, and I didn't know how to say it. I didn't want to say it, because I felt like that would have opened up a can of worms. This woman seemed to have a question for every question and the answer from me was, *I don't know.* I didn't know how to pray anymore. I didn't know how to talk to God, or if He was even listening to me after all the wrongs I'd done.

Tonight, at the table when Presley was praying over the food, I was almost moved to tears. I couldn't believe the words that came out of her mouth so easily about God not leaving or forsaking her though, she didn't deserve His grace. How did she know that I needed to hear those things? Thoughts raced through my head as my heart longed for answers.

So, I went upstairs. And I got on my knees, which felt like a pretty good place to start. And I prayed. At least, I think I did. It was more of a "hello" to God and a long pause to see if He would answer. But, in a way, I think He already had. Perhaps, He was sending me signs through this woman. Maybe He was telling me to work on my patience, because if I was not, how could He extend patience to me? But, I was noticing that this woman's questions, her humming, and the fact that she was now blasting some of my favorite songs through my house—none of that irritated me. In fact, I was enjoying the company. I'd been lonely. And that feeling had been exacerbated since I was so far from God. But, according to Presley, I was not far at all.

As I sat on my knees in a dark room, with my eyes closed shut, I didn't let my mind wander. I wanted to focus as hard as I could on listening, which was something I had never been good at.

It may have been the downfall to my last relationship, my lack of listening. I certainly wasn't good at picking up cues either. Poppy talked *a lot* and after a while, I just couldn't keep up with it all. My own thoughts became muddled with hers, because she spoke every one of them, but would quiz me later on what she said. At first, I took it as a gentle nudge that I should listen and cherish her words. Her voice was like an angel singing, and I was the blessed one for being the recipient of such poetry that she spoke. Later on, the words became harder to interpret. She would say things like "so-and-so's boyfriend took her to Paris" or "Tanya's husband listens to her." But all the flights in the world wouldn't have fixed things at that point, and I was absolutely clueless about that because it was then and there that I booked us a trip, where I was planning on asking her if she wanted to elope. I even ordered a custom wedding ring set that couldn't be returned, which was delivered shortly after she left me.

No, I'd never been good at listening. But God was, and I knew He was just waiting for me to speak. To repent. To turn from those ways that I'd already written off so long ago. TO tell Him about my plan for dating—that I would not pursue a relationship again that He had not ordained. I wanted to say these things. I had felt these words crawling around in my head and heart for the last several months. However, the words didn't come to me.

After a long while, I got up and decided to shower since I was already up here. While I was in the shower, with the hot water beating down on my face and cold skin, the tune of the music blaring in the background, I called out to God.

"Lord, please forgive me! Come back to me, God! Show me the ways that a godly man should live and straighten my paths that I may follow You!" And I wept for the first time since my mother died all those years ago.

*****

As I ambled down the stairs of my chalet that evening, I was in my head talking to God with every step. I felt relief; a weight I had been carrying for so long was lifted from my shoulders. Guilt was gone. Shame was gone. Joy was returning.

The song that was playing on the record player was a catchy tune, and I automatically started humming to the music as I walked over to my magnificent picture window. I felt myself bursting with thankfulness for everything I had; God's grace abounded in my life, despite my not deserving it.

Turning, I saw Presley at the table putting together a jigsaw puzzle in her leggings and ski shirt. I looked at her from where I stood, before she acknowledged me, as she was lost in her puzzle. She was a beautiful woman, probably about my age. I didn't know much about her, but I thought back to my promise I made about women. I found myself saying another prayer in my mind to tell God about that promise. I would be as respectful of God's boundaries as I was with Presley. Despite this forced proximity, I would honor the Lord with my actions and words.

As if on cue, Presley spoke. As she held her hand out to me with the invitation to dance, I was stunned. What kind of gentleman turns down a lady's offer to dance with her? After contemplating this for a moment and hearing the tune, which was possibly my favorite Elvis song of all time, I accepted.

Presley walked over to me, and I met her in the middle of the living room. She took my left hand in her right, and I carefully placed my other hand on her upper back. There was more than enough room in between us and after swaying for a moment, she looked up at me and smiled. I didn't realize it until now just how much shorter than me Presley was. I was around six foot one, and Presley must have been ten inches shorter than me. I never stood close enough to her until just now to notice.

Feeling my body relax and with the realization that I didn't want to do anything that might dishonor God, I released the breath I was holding in. This was just dancing, until it wasn't, and I would make sure that it didn't go beyond this. *Make sure it doesn't, Lord.* I let go of my hand on her back and held her out with one hand, and she did a spin. It was then that I remembered that this cowboy loved to dance.

Two twirls and a dip later, I felt the plot thicken between us. As the song ended, she thanked me for the dance, and I found myself filled with gratitude that she asked me. It was enjoyable and with my boundaries in place, nothing else happened. She was full of laughter and went back to the dining room table.

I followed and picked up the box of the puzzle to see what she was creating—a snowy, ski slope landscape with little glitter accents.

"It glows in the dark, too," she said with a coy smile. Her eyes looking up at me from the table made a twinge in my chest. Presley was radiant—that was obvious to anyone who glanced her way—but I was just now noticing to the degree that she was.

"Very cool. Mind if I join? I don't think I've done a puzzle since I was a kid. My grandmother used to have them going on a card table permanently set up in her living room. Right next to that bowl of strawberry candy." As I reminisced aloud, Presley chimed in.

"I love that candy. I buy it sometimes," she laughed.

"You can buy it? I've never seen it in stores," I said, confused.

"Well, it's not delivered by the stork the day someone becomes a grandmother. Of course you can buy it, silly!" she teased and tossed a puzzle piece at my head. I was so caught off guard at her playfulness, I didn't even know what to say. So, I flicked one back at her, and it poked her in the eye.

"Oh my, I'm so sorry, Presley. I didn't mean to—" I stammered, and she started laughing.

"Good shot, Ford. I'll remember that next time I shouldn't go easy on you. Careful though, I can be ruthless with a piece of sticky bubblegum in a slingshot," she giggled, taking a sip of her tea as she started to slowly put a few pieces together.

"So," I started, not knowing how to finish the sentence. "Tell me about. . . something. Tell me about *you.*" It was as good a start as any. She looked surprised at my conversation, and I was certain it was because I'd been such a silent dud around her these last few days.

"I'm a book publisher in Denver, and I'm here because I just about snapped at work. Well, I think I had a meltdown right before work, but it was a prolonged reaction. I've been very overworked and *under vacationed* in the last. . . five years." Presley didn't waste any time jumping right into her story that she shared so easily. The woman was transparent, and I wasn't sure how to handle that. I'd never been around a woman who told me what she was thinking instead of saying something different and making me guess. As she went on, I found myself captivated with what she had to say, and I also started to realize I'd been trying to maintain control of every situation, when in fact, my life had been in God's hands all along. Wasn't that the very thing I just prayed for? "I crammed to the limits in college so I could graduate early, and I went right to work. No gap year, no time off. A nervous breakdown was inevitable at some point, and I happened to have it this week." She gave a smile with her thumbs in the air, and I laughed. "So, that's how I ended up here for a week. In Sage Mountain, during a power outage, and a major incoming storm. I can't wait to see what lesson this turns out to be, because God really does have a sense of humor."

"That He does," I said, as I watched her animated expressions while she spoke. She certainly had my full attention—she was entertaining as all get out. A little noise came from Priscilla, and Presley jumped up.

"Did you finish that already?" she asked, getting down on the ground to check out her dog's toy. "I filled this with the tiniest bit of peanut butter—kept her entertained for at least an hour!" Presley exclaimed. The dog looked dang proud of herself as she licked her little lips clean.

"Cute," I said, surprising myself. *Cute?* I know I had prayed to be a changed man but did I really just say that out loud? *God, have You softened me up that much already?* Looking at the dog, Priscilla, I couldn't deny that she was adorable. This evening, she was sporting a purple sweater and had two matching bows in her hair. Presley must have changed her outfit from earlier because I didn't remember it. Or maybe, I was just too self-absorbed to notice. Probably the latter.

Presley brought over a fluffy dog bed for Priscilla to sit in while she returned to the puzzle, but instead, the dog went and got a drink at the tiniest little dog bowl I'd ever seen next to the kitchen island. It was so small, I didn't think I would have noticed it otherwise—probably the size of my palm. As she got what sounded like a much-needed drink, the record started winding down. If I recalled correctly, there were maybe three songs left before it needed to be flipped. It was already dark outside, and the day was catching up to me. I decided at the end of this record, I would go to bed.

"Now, tell me about you, Ford," Presley smiled.

"Well, there's not much to tell that you probably don't already know," I said, considering she'd been my roommate for two days.

"Try me."

"Let's see. I'm a skijorer. Been doing that since I was about nine years old." She nodded, signaling that she wanted more. "I won a national championship a few years ago, and that's what qualified me for the Winter Games. Now, I'm just competing in those, pretty much. With brand deals, I stay pretty busy, which is awesome." I was quickly running out of material to give her. A sliver of doubt made me wonder if she had already looked me up online and knew about Poppy and the shameful breakup. I shook that thought from my mind, reminding myself that the devil wanted me to feel shame and doubt, not God.

"What about you? What else do you like to do? Skiing, of course." As she pressed, I started to think outside of skijoring.

"It's a hard question to answer, because skijoring is the thing that has all but consumed every inch of my life for the last decade. Kind of like how you said about publishing." Her eyes widened.

"Thank you for sharing. And listening to me," she said. It wasn't lost on me how low the bar was set for this woman, but

I was one of the worst offenders for not listening, so I just nodded. It was clear that we both had been through some rough experiences with the opposite sex, and I'd leave it at that if she did. "I totally get it. I always wanted so much more in life, but the success of my career trumped it. I no longer had time for anything that wasn't publishing. Sometimes I think I'd trade it all for a family," she said, hiding behind her words as she pretended to analyze the puzzle box. Little did she know, I felt her pain. In the next room, my computer let out a familiar chime.

"Excuse me. I didn't realize the computer was still on. It does this annoying thing whenever I get an email," I joked and walked to the office.

Pulling up a browser, I checked my messages. The property management company I used had replied to my previous email about Presley's chalet. The bad news was they wouldn't be able to fix that fireplace issue so easily. It was going to have to be a project for late spring, when contractors could come up and fix things properly. The good news was they had an opening for a no-show in chalet #5. The guests couldn't make it due to the roads being closed down.

I read the email with a mixed bag of emotions. The woman I was hosting here in my home had somewhere else to go. Surely, they were going to reach out to her next and let her know. How would she react? Would she be anxious to leave, to get away from me? For some reason, I wanted her to stay here with me. I wasn't proud of it, but for a moment, I contemplated simply omitting the fact there was another option for her lodging. *Jesus, help me.* Not telling her would be slimy, and a hostage situation. All I could do was come clean. And that's exactly what I'd do.

Returning to the table that was now covered with a nearly-completed puzzle border, I spilled the beans.

"That was the property management company. There is nothing they can do about your chalet; it will require much more extensive repairs, unfortunately. But chalet #5 is open because the guests couldn't get here. Though the power might be out, it does have a working fireplace, if you'd like to have your own space again." The look on her face was familiar. While I'd never been a good interpreter, I sensed that she wanted to know what I wanted out of the situation. So, I added something in. "Of course, I think it's fun having you here if you'd like to stay, you know, with electricity and all that." She smiled and nodded.

"Yeah, if it's no problem, I don't think I want to be walking around with a flashlight. Unless the power turns back on, of course," Presley nodded to herself.

"Of course," I said back. Though I found myself praying that it wouldn't.

Almost everywhere in Sage Mountain had generators. The fact that my brand-new chalets were lacking them was almost a little embarrassing. I was just glad I had thought to get mine installed before moving in. But, as long as the ski resort could stay open for all of this fresh snow, I didn't care. I had enough diesel reserves to run the generator for a month if it came down to it.

As I lingered in the chalet, wondering if I should join her back at the table or remove myself from the room altogether, a foreign noise came from the back bedroom, *Presley's room.* Presley heard it too, as she stood up and paused.

"What was that?" she asked. We were both on high alert as we walked to the room. At first, nothing seemed out of place. Her bed was made so well, the sheets had to have been ironed. None of her things were out except for her phone charging on the nightstand. The room smelled like a bouquet of flowers, which must have been Presley's perfume. I would have known if I had stood that close to her, but I didn't plan on it anytime soon because of *boundaries.* But then, I took one step inside.

"The window is broken!" Presley called out, pointing to a large crack in the glass. "Do you have any duct tape?" The window was so large that I didn't think that tape could fix it, but I didn't want to discourage her idea, either—something that an hour ago I wouldn't have considered.

"I think I have a roll in my garage. Let me go check," I said, tearing out of the chalet. What on earth could have broken that window? I decided to take a quick trek around the chalet to see if I could see anything out of the ordinary. But first, I needed a flashlight.

My garage had a lot of random things in it; some of the remaining construction materials from all of the chalets had been stored there, hence, why I didn't park in it yet. I needed time to go through it and see what was what. Miraculously, I found a large, yellow flashlight sitting right next to a fresh roll of duct tape. "Thank you, Lord!" The praise came to me so naturally, I didn't think about it. Joy, through this hiccup, was possible. I left the garage to do a quick perimeter search around the building before going back inside.

All of the chalets were three stories; you had your garage at the street level; the front door up some heated concrete steps, so no slipping on ice; and then inside, there was an upstairs loft. I loved the design because I could see more mountain peaks and chairlifts this way. I could tell if some of my favorite runs were groomed without pulling it up on the internet. But right now in the dark, with the chalet towering above me, I found the design adding difficulty to determining what exactly went wrong here.

Then, I saw it: A tree branch had broken from the snowfall and was waving in the wind, hitting the chalet with every breeze. I surmised a large gust pushed it hard into the chalet. Since it was still attached and could fall at any moment, and I was standing under it, I hightailed it out of there and went back inside, while my boot prints were filling back up with powder as soon as I made them.

"It's that tree branch, right there." I pointed to it out the window, holding the flashlight so Presley could see it outside.

"Oh no! I hope it doesn't hit the window again. Do you think there's anyone who can come fix that tonight, so it doesn't?" A loud crack sounded as the branch swung back at the chalet, making us both jump. Presley screamed and her body fell into mine in fear. For a moment, we were in an embrace; I stiffened, knowing that temptation was real. She whispered an apology and took a few steps away. I paused, but I didn't want to make a big deal out of it, so I answered her question.

"I'm really not sure, but the snow is still falling. I doubt I could get an emergency tree trimmer tonight." If only I had a forklift, I could fix the thing by myself. I thought about Presley in this room with that tree tonight. Even after we taped the windows, the cold air was still seeping through. "You can take my bedroom until we get this fixed properly. I'll take the couch," I said, walking out of the room. As if on cue, Priscilla jumped up on the couch and started wagging her tail. "Someone has already got my spot warmed up."

"You don't have to do that, Ford. I'm already staying here, taking up space in your chalet. I'll take the couch. Priscilla wants to sleep on it anyway—she's making that clear." We both smirked at how she was acting as she ran around the couch cushions and sporadically began digging on the blanket.

"I insist. I'd rather stay down here to monitor if the window gets hit again." Presley looked like she was weighing her options. Her comment about taking up space didn't sit well with me.

"Okay, if you promise you don't mind." I shook my head, going to the linen closet off the laundry room to grab some fresh sheets and pillowcases. Presley had set her luggage at the end of the stairs, so I brought it up with me. By the time I made it upstairs to strip the bed, Presley had taken another bag up there and was putting her beauty products around my sink. A bark from the bottom of the stairs got her attention.

"Priscilla hates stairs. She tripped on one when she was a puppy and has held a grudge ever since," she said. My back was turned to Presley, and I felt a smile coming on. Who would have thought that Shih Tzu's were so *entertaining?*

After the sheets were changed, I went back downstairs to where Presley was back at the table with her dog on her lap.

"I thought I'd work on this a few more minutes before bed. Want to join me?" Every part of my being was ready to go to sleep, but there we were in my makeshift bedroom for the night. I didn't want to be rude to my guest, so I walked over to the table and sat down. Presley had quite a bit of the puzzle in progress already. "This helps me unwind and think a little clearer before I go to sleep. Usually, I read before bed, but I've sworn off anything that isn't the Bible for this week." She smiled and looked at me, waiting for me to jump into the conversation. "You must pay for every word that comes out of your mouth, huh?"

"What do you mean?" I shook my head in confusion.

"I mean, you don't say much. That's okay, because I've been told I say a lot." She shrugged her shoulders.

"It's their loss, Presley." I couldn't stop the words coming out of my mouth if I tried. "It sounds like the men you've dated have been real jerks." Her jaw dropped and eyebrows raised.

"I mean, that's what I was leaning towards too but. . . Thank you for saying that," she said. We sat in silence for a few minutes, and I finally found the correct puzzle piece to fit into the perimeter. "Good job, Ford," she said, getting up and pushing her chair into the table, Priscilla in her arm. "Well, thanks for the chat. Goodnight." As she turned, I watched her walk up the stairs and into my bedroom.

That night, I took a top sheet and threw it over the couch. Using an extra comforter to keep warm, I dozed off quickly and only awoke at the sound of a tree branch tapping the window in the guest bedroom. *Presley's room.* I got up a few times to make sure the glass was secure, but thanks to the tape, it appeared it was going to hold. There wasn't much of a draft coming in, despite the hasty tape job, which was a relief. As I paced back to the living room, I considered what could happen if the chalet got too cold. Or if the generator went out. I threw a couple logs in my wood burning fireplace and watched the fire tear through the fire starters and then into the logs. The popping noises and familiar scent brought back memories of my childhood on a ranch in southern Wyoming.

I used to go out on cattle drives with my dad and his ranching buddies in the summer. The cows had to be moved to places where they could have fresh land to graze; it took several days to do so, as it required them walking to where we needed them to go. We didn't have the means to transport them like some of the other fancy ranches around. So, sometimes that required sleeping in the middle of a large pasture, out in the middle of nowhere. I secretly loved being out in the wilderness sleeping, though my dad always complained about it.

His back would hurt from sleeping on the ground, even if he brought a three-inch thick piece of memory foam out with us. And he'd miss my mother's cooking and long to be away from food that came in a can. But I loved it. I always wanted to show him my fire building skills, how I could ride on the horse like him and his friends just as well, or that I perfected the art of cooking a hot dog over a fire. He never seemed to care. I wondered if Clint had been the one showing him all of these things, would he have felt differently? But Clint was always back home overseeing the ranch, irrigating. Digging ditches. Or mending fences.

Even when I got caught by a tree branch while on a runaway horse as a kid, giving me a permanent, deep scar in my jaw line, I didn't think he noticed. I'd never forget that day; he grudgingly took me to the emergency room. They gave me fifteen crude stitches, making X marks all down it. As it healed, I wasn't allowed to play outside because they didn't want the bills that would follow if it became infected. In my hurt, I felt like a burden to them.

Now, in my adulthood, I realized I had never connected on an emotional level with my family, and that was difficult for a child to experience. Especially when my older brother, Clint, was the golden child. Did they even want children? I wondered that, but their reaction to my brother's every waking breath said otherwise. What they did want was help around their farm, and society had certain expectations of people. Or, at least they did back then. I'd like to have believed that they tried their best or did what they could, but I wasn't sure what they were capable of because they never showed me. As I lay listening to the fire crackle, its warmth spreading throughout my body, I realized I'd been holding a grudge against my brother for receiving what I didn't. Because I didn't receive the love I had wanted, now I wasn't forgiving him for it.

Lord, I need your help to forgive. Within seconds of my prayer, I was fast asleep once again.

When morning came, I was awake at dawn. The soft glow of the sun was reflecting light off of all the new snow that came overnight. It was touchingly beautiful, and I had the urge to call my brother for the first time in years. *God, is this forgiveness?* If only my phone wasn't broken. I went to my computer and quickly typed up a request to my manager, Jack, and asked if he could have a new one sent to me when the roads opened.

Then, I went to freshen up in the guest bathroom. I had brought my toothbrush and toothpaste down here last night, but I had forgotten my razor and shaving cream. I felt my stubble; it was already unruly. I wasn't the type of man who had a 5 o'clock shadow the same day, but my facial hair seemed to always be present in the mornings.

Changing into my ski clothes, I decided I'd spend one more day on the slopes before the Winter Games. Originally, I thought about just using today as a rest and recharge day, but sitting around all day long inside did nothing but bring me anxiety and worry. I'd been learning that about myself over the years; idle hands give the enemy too much to work with. At least for me. While I wasn't running from reality—in fact, I had my best thoughts while doing tasks—I couldn't stay here.

In the laundry room, I slipped on my ski pants over my long johns. The henley long sleeve shirt I wore felt like it shrunk in the dryer. I made a mental note to get another one ordered soon. A door opened upstairs, followed by Presley carrying her dog down.

"Good morning," she said, her eyes looking fresh and bright. Priscilla was in a bright pink sweater as Presley stopped to put a coat and boots on them both before going outside.

"How did you sleep?" I asked, out of character for myself. Or was it?

"We slept great, thanks for asking. The heat from the fire just lulled us to sleep like angels. And you? I'm sorry you had to give up your nice bed for the couch."

"It was fine. I liked it. And I'm happy to report, the window didn't get hit again. Yet, anyway," I said. She smiled.

"Oh, thank goodness. I kept thinking I heard something creaking out there. I know I've been here a few days, so you'd think I'd be used to all the sounds of Sage Mountain. But I still wake up and wonder where I am."

"That's probably because you've slept in a different bed every night you've been here." I crossed my arms and gave her a knowing look.

"You're so right about that." She tapped her forehead as if to say, "duh." Presley looked me up and down. "So, training again today?" I shook my head.

"Nah. It's all done. I've prepared all that I can for the Winter Games. Today, I wasn't planning on it, but I've decided to go skiing again."

"Ah, so there will be a tiger on the slopes today?" Presley laughed, and I nodded.

"It's the only way I can be left alone." I looked at her. Her hair was in a braid going down her shoulder blades, and she was wearing her ski clothes and a fitted black turtleneck. I didn't know makeup well, but I could tell she was wearing a pink lip gloss. I found myself thinking of her lips. *Ford—get a grip.* It was hardly seven in the morning.

"I bet it gets crazy with people recognizing you all the time. How long has that been happening?" she asked. I thought about it for a moment.

"Probably the last five years or so. Things really exploded again when I was in a high-profile relationship with my ex." Just bringing Poppy up made me feel weird. But, God had forgiven me, and I had been freed from the shame and grief of that time in my life.

"I see. Well, I'm glad you have such a good disguise. It certainly worked for you when we were in the gondola when that woman was fawning over you, and no one was the wiser." I waited for the questions about my ex to come, but they didn't. I knew she wanted to ask, because in my experience, every woman wants to know the details of past relationships. But it dawned on me: Presley wasn't interested in me like that, and that was okay.

Not to sound full of myself, or like I assumed she would be, but I'd always been a little bit of a lady's man. But, since Poppy, I'd turned into a private recluse who steered clear of any and all women. It had been a relatively long stretch that I hadn't even considered the idea of talking to a woman beyond friendship, and suddenly, here I was, toying with the idea if this woman liked me.

CHAPTER 7: PRESLEY

THE TIGER UNMASKED

I slept well in Ford's comfortable bed. He had one of those firm mattresses with the cooling pillowtop on it. If it wasn't for waking at every little movement downstairs from him or his fireplace, I would have been out like a light. But the truth was, my awareness of Ford was growing quickly. Last night, I even prayed about it. "Lord, what is happening here?' "I asked. Either God was working through me to reach Ford, or Ford was starting to reach me. And that was both terrifying and exciting at the same time.

I still knew very little about Ford, other than the fact he was drop-dead handsome, of course. And turned out, a great dancer. I had my guard up pretty strong last night, but there was a moment when he dipped me, I felt something in my heart. My feelings for him were solidified in a way. Seeing him up close, yet, out of the kissing distance, my heart was fawning over him.

I respected how gentlemanly he was being and hoped it was because he was starting to like me. So, with my phone back and charged, I did a few web searches of him last night. I watched race videos. Interviews. Saw pictures. And then I read the bios of the people who were in—or had been previously—involved in his life. Including his ex-fiancé, Poppy.

Before I knew it, I was in one of those message boards that were dedicated to him. It was made up of mostly women who thought he was gorgeous but some fans of his skijoring, too. One of the posts caught my attention: ***Ford's ex fiancé gets married to Sage Mountain CEO.*** Suddenly, I felt like I was reading something I shouldn't. It was too personal and almost creepy to be learning this much about a person who was just right downstairs. If only I could have asked him. He may not have seemed like an open book right now, but for the time being, he had graciously allowed me to be his roommate. Heck, I was even using his bedroom, and he was on the couch.

My convictions led me to put the phone down. This person was showing me boundless kindness by allowing me and my high maintenance Shih Tzu, Priscilla, who was acting as if he was the only man she'd ever seen, stay with him. The least I could have done was stop reading about his deeply personal wounds online.

After I turned it off and went to sleep, I awoke this morning and started to think of Ford in a different light. There was more to this brooding exterior than what met the eye, I was certain of it. Remembering a video where he and Poppy were being interviewed at a sporting event, he seemed so doting. Caring. Kind. Now, I picked up on those things but also a deep hesitation. Last night, as I fell asleep, I said another prayer about Ford that he could forgive those who hurt him. And that maybe, he could find someone who would protect his heart at all costs.

As I did my hair and brushed my teeth for the day before going downstairs with Priscilla, I considered all of this praying I'd been doing for Ford. My heart sank. "Lord, I'm afraid I've started to fall for this man, and I don't want to do that again unless it's for the man I'm going to marry. Lord, turn these feelings off. Please don't let me get hurt."

A calm feeling came over me as I put on a light tinted moisturizer and found myself taking a little extra time for a sparkle shadow on my lids and a minor eyebrow shaping. I looked to the bed where Priscilla was still snoring; she wasn't waiting on me. I had plenty of time to take care of myself before the lifts started running. I braided my hair and decided a little lip gloss wouldn't hurt either; it might just help protect my lips from getting chapped.

After several minutes, I put down the makeup and woke up Priscilla. She rolled on her back so I could scratch her tummy, which I happily obliged. Then, when she was ready, she rolled back over and let me put a sweater on her. Today, I chose a bright pink frock with small matching hair clips for her pigtails. It was so adorable that I picked her up and kissed her on the head out of joy. *Thank You God for dogs! They bring so much happiness to our lives.*

As we headed downstairs, I nearly stopped in my tracks when I saw Ford. He was wearing a skintight, long sleeved henley, and I wasn't mad about it. His muscles appeared to be *very* well defined, no doubt thanks to his sport and that gym he had set up in his third bedroom. We had some idle morning chat as I prepared to take Priscilla outside, and when I returned, it continued some more. I noticed he seemed much more talkative as the days went by. Was he opening up to me, perhaps?

Before I knew it, Poppy came up in conversation, and my mind was fending off the guilt from already knowing about it. I didn't press, though he left plenty of opportunity to ask questions, and I thought maybe that made me appear like a *cool* chick that wasn't overbearing with questions. But in reality, my mind had tons of them. "Overbearing" was my nickname in college from a guy named Ben who went out with me a total of two times after he brought up a woman that he wanted to ask out on a date, and I mentioned the fact that he was already on a date with me. He said, "I didn't realize that meant we were married," to which, I objected that we would in fact, never be. That was hurtful.

Another nickname was "Spreadsheet" after I made a few for my chemistry lab partner in high school, so he could keep our projects organized. Despite him telling me that was the only way he passed that class—and graduated, because he was on very thin ice academically—he coined the term, and it caught on with all of his football buddy friends.

So now, as I was looking around for a pen so that I could cover the contents of Ford's refrigerator in sticky notes asking for further details, "Is this organic?" or "Eat this soon—it expires in a week," my stomach growled again, interrupting my quest.

"Should I make us some breakfast? Or did you already eat?" I asked him.

"I haven't eaten yet, but how about I cook for you?" he asked, to which I couldn't say no.

"Okay, that sounds really nice," I smiled, and I found myself taking this personally. Did he want to cook for me? Was I reading into this too far? Was he falling for me? I collected Priscilla's food out of the fridge. She had been glued to Ford's ankles since we came back inside.

"Are you hungry, sweetie?" I asked, to which she galloped over to her bowl and ate.

"What a ferocious little thing," Ford commented, as he took a mix out of the cupboard. Filling a pan with water, he began to boil it. "Do you like eggs benedict?" he asked, which was music to my ears.

"Like it? I *love* it! It's my favorite breakfast." He smiled and nodded.

"Mine too," he whispered. It was so faint that I almost didn't hear it. Sitting down at the table, I put a few more puzzle pieces together while I sipped on some hot coffee. Colors from the sunrise caught my attention and soon, I was glued to the picture window, watching the beautiful alpenglow of God's creation.

Breakfast was whipped up fast. Within ten minutes, I had two beautiful poached eggs on perfectly crisped English muffins coated with a heaping amount of hollandaise sauce.

"Would you like to join me in prayer?" I asked, considering how yesterday I had sprung it on him without considering if he might. Ford gave a hesitant nod, and I reached my hand out to him, clasping his.

"Dear heavenly Father, we thank You for this blessing of food this morning. And for the bountiful heaps of snow that You have graced us with. May this food energize our bodies and keep us strong, and may You protect us from harm on the slopes. In Your name, Amen."

"Amen," Ford croaked out as we released each other's hands. As I took a bite of the food, I almost fell backward.

"This is the *best* eggs benedict I have ever had!" I savored the bite, tasting the tangy sauce with the perfectly gooey egg. It was divine.

"Thanks. It's the only breakfast food I really know how to make from scratch," he shrugged.

"And you're doing it well, my friend." As we ate, I still felt the weight of his hand in mine. I was trying not to think about how rugged it felt to my soft, slender hands. Or the strength that it gave off. No, I wouldn't daydream of this man's masculine attributes as I was sitting next to him. As I was staying with him in his chalet. As I was camped out in his bedroom while he took the couch.

As if on cue, Priscilla, being the diva that she was, jumped up from the floor into Ford's lap while he was eating. The look of surprise on his face when she did that made me break out into a gut-wrenching laugh.

"I'm so sorry. Clearly, I've enabled this behavior," I said as I got up to put her back on the floor. But Ford just shrugged.

"This has been a long time coming. I'm okay with it," he smiled, and I started laughing again. The sight of this rugged, manly cowboy with my Shih Tzu wearing a pink sweater and pig tails sitting on his lap was all that my heart could handle. The joy was overwhelming as I finished my delicious meal, and we chatted about Priscilla. *Lord, I can't help it. I've fallen for this man.*

Priscilla's Inner Monologue

Darling, I rather like this man we are accompanying this week. He has hands large enough to transport me and our luggage,

I offered to clear the table while Ford went to get ready for his day. After taking her outside one more time, Priscilla found her favorite spot on the couch: in the blanket that Ford used for sleeping last night. It appeared I was not the only one with a huge crush on this man. As we both readied for skiing, he turned to look at me.

"Would you like to go skiing. . . with me?" My heart bounced at his words. I wanted to shout from the rooftops, proclaiming my answer. I felt like one of those old-timey showgirls who would do those synchronized kicks to the music. I felt like I could fly.

"Yes, I would!" my answer was a little too eager, with both tone and *volume.* He looked at me like I about blew his hair back when I responded, but after a moment, he smiled and nodded. *Whew.*

We left the chalet and headed for the gondola. I had my skis over my shoulder on one arm and was carrying my ski poles in the other, but after I got to the sidewalk off his driveway, he stopped me.

"Here, give me the skis. You can carry the poles." His chivalry was refreshing. I obliged, watching him throw a set of skis over each shoulder and carry them effortlessly. As we got closer to the gondola line, skiers were being turned away.

"What's going on?" I asked a skier who was walking the opposite direction of the gondola.

"The power is still out at the resort, too. The transformer blew, so now they are limiting the number of skiers because they can only run so many lifts." A look of concern came over my face, as I hoped we would be let in. Clearly, this person wasn't, so I didn't get my hopes up.

"Thank you for the information," I said to the woman as we went our separate ways. "What do you think we should do?" I asked Ford, who was wearing his tiger mask again.

"Let's still give it a try. Look at all of these people turning away, assuming they won't get in. By the time we make it through the line, we just might." And that's exactly what happened. The line moved quickly, because people were giving up waiting for another gondola to move. The resort was limiting skiers based on the type of lift ticket you had—Ford and I both had season passes, which according to today's rules, weren't being able to ski. But, with a quick flash of Ford's face to the man running the lift, he let us in the gondola. Not only that, but we were riding it alone.

"Gee," I said, the moment we were up in the air. "It's so fun skiing with someone famous," I razzed him, and he shrugged, taking his mask down for the time being since we were alone.

"I know that was rather. . . tacky of me. But I really wanted to ski with you today." His words brought more excitement to my heart than I cared to admit.

"Well, I did too. So, thank you for revealing your identity. You can now go back to being the mysterious tiger man." I looked out the window, searching the snowy canyons below us for moose.

"Are you comfortable with blues and blacks?" Ford asked, in reference to which ski runs I wanted to take.

"Yeah, pretty much anything that isn't moguls. My knees just hate moguls. Oh, and ice. That's hard to ski on no matter what level of run. I also don't like it when it's super steep the whole way. A little steep is fine, maybe going into the run, but—" I paused to consider my words to make sure I was describing it correctly. "So, yes. As long as the conditions are perfect, I am comfortable with intermediate to advanced runs." I smiled. I didn't like that I couldn't see his face, and he could see mine. "You know. . . if no one is up here, maybe you don't need to wear the mask. Just sayin'."

"I was thinking that same thing," he said as he pulled it down, revealing his devastatingly handsome jawline. It somehow looked even better while he wore his ski goggles and helmet.

"That's better. Now, I can see your face." *And what a face it was.* He looked like he was chiseled from stone. I didn't mean for the words to sound like they did, but I shrugged it off, remembering I promised the Lord I wouldn't cower from who I was. I was silly, goofy and a little awkward sometimes, and that was okay. *All the best people are.* He smirked back at me.

As the gondola slowed to let us out at the top, I jumped out but somehow, Ford still beat me to the skis. He grabbed both pairs and walked over to the starting point, setting mine down for me first. Quite the gentlemen, which was a nice change from the men I'd been around in the last few years. I was forced to remind myself that Ford was not a man I was dating, but rather one who was probably just trying to keep the peace because we' were forced to live together until further notice.

"Want to look at the map, or do you know your way around the mountain?" I asked him. His goggles were down, and he expertly clipped into his skis in two seconds flat.

"I'm pretty familiar with things, but if you want to look, go ahead," he shrugged. I veered over to the map to the right, not entirely sure what I was looking for. There were no mountain hosts working today to give me a route, but I could just trust Ford to show me around and not be such a control freak. Was that even possible?

"Okay, I'll let you be the guide today. Where do you want to ski?" I asked him.

"My favorite run when there is this much fresh powder is Great Big World. You'll love it—it skis right through a forest of trees and ends at a diner where they make really good hot chocolate."

"Ahh, my favorite kind of skiing is when there are treats involved." I gleefully got my ski legs and followed him as we took off.

It was clear from the moment he disembarked that he was the best skier I'd ever seen. His body was able to lean at a 90-degree angle while he carved through the fresh powder and made turns, without falling over. If I even attempted that, I'd have ended up in a full body cast. Ford moved so fluidly; it looked like he wasn't outputting any energy whatsoever. Watching him inspired my own skiing as I started trying to improve my intermediate skills by following his tracks. After a few minutes, I was so out of breath I had to stop and rest my legs.

"I'm sorry; this is amazing, but I don't usually work so hard at my turns," I said, embarrassingly winded. I sounded like I was fighting for my life as I choked the words out. I felt like it, too.

"Yikes, I didn't mean to go so fast. I'll slow down," he winced, pulling up his goggles as he looked all around us for other people.

"No, don't slow down. This is really good for me. Skill building. You can never stop improving. Once you do, you're dead—" I was interrupted as Ford ambled towards me, pushing me out of the way and down on the ground, nearly falling on top of me.

"Watch out!" a snowboarder yelled as he slid down the mountain right past us at lightning speed on his rear end.

"Are you okay?" Ford asked, his face mere inches from mine. His lips were so… kissable at this moment, I almost forgot I had a face full of snow.

"Yes, I think so. Thank you. Getting hit by a snowboarder was not on my bingo card today." Ford hesitated, his face still nearly touching mine, and I closed my eyes, my lips instinctively forming into a pout. Was he going to kiss me or leave me out in the cold? After a moment where nothing but snow was touching my lips, I opened my eyes again. Ford looked like he was closing in, ready to kiss me. Then, at the last second, he sat up, and I was reminded by the Lord that I had just asked Him to protect my heart from getting hurt. So, why now was I hoping to be kissed by this cowboy?

Using his ski pole to launch himself to his skis, he reached out a hand to help me up. I took his gloved hand in mine as he easily lifted me to my feet, but my mind forgot I was on two waxed skis, as each leg decided to go in a different direction. I let out a whimper while my legs tried to do the splits, but the only split I was worried about was in the back of my pants.

"Yikes!" I hollered, grabbing onto Ford's broad shoulders to regain my stance. I put my legs back to where they should have been and let go of him. "I'm sorry, I lost my footing there for a second." He looked like he wanted to laugh but didn't.

"You, uh, ready to go?" We'd only been skiing for a few minutes and already, I'd made a scene.

"Giddy up," I said, to which he stared at me. I couldn't tell if his eyes were rolling since his goggles were reflecting back at me, but I'd have put money on it that they were. "I mean, let's go, cowboy." Ugh. *So cringe.*

Ford motioned for me to lead the way. "Ladies first." I appreciated that as it let me set the speed and tone for the day, but I felt like I was holding him up. So, I started to push my limits and ski faster, which miraculously made my turns a little more effortless. Before I knew it, I was leaning into the angles like they were nothing, shredding through the snow almost as fast as Ford was earlier. At the end of the run, I came to a slow as the mountain top cafe was in my sights. *"Top of the World Cafe"* was illuminated in large lettering above the floor to ceiling glass windows. I turned, grinning ear to ear to see if Ford was as excited as I was to get a hot chocolate, but he was nowhere to be found.

"What the heck? Ford? Where did you go?" I called out. A second later, I saw a skier in the distance coming off of a jump made out of snow to the side. As he landed effortlessly in the soft, pillowy snow, he was smiling back at me.

"Sorry, I can never resist that little side run. It's short and mainly just a leadup to that jump, but it's my favorite." He was panting from the adrenaline of it all as we unclipped our skis. "You're a great skier, by the way," he said under his breath.

"Thank you. That was probably the best I've ever skied. Turns out I just needed to pick up the pace all of these years. Going behind you really got my butt in gear." He slid his tiger mask back up over his jawline, his mouth still exposed. *His lips were almost begging me to kiss them,* I thought to myself. Ugh! *Lord, please keep my feelings—and my thoughts—platonic and honoring You.*

As we walked up to the cafe, I considered the current forced-roommate situation. In the very least, if I couldn't fend off my feelings that were growing for this man by the second, let me at least keep my wits and dignity. The last thing I needed was another let down. Every bone in my body was telling me to not date again because every man I'd ever been involved with had hurt me in one way or another, and just recently, I had made the decision to swear off dating. But my heart yearned for love. To be a wife. To have children. In a world that glorified sin and all things that lead to a life of unfulfillment, it was a tough spot to be in.

"What would you like, Presley? My treat." Ford looked at me as I glanced at the menu.

"If they recognize you, do I get extra marshmallows?" I asked, to which he cracked a smile. "How about a vanilla mocha and a triple chocolate scone?" He nodded. "Or, actually, I'll get an apple cider with that pumpkin fritter right there. That glaze just looks heavenly," I said as I pointed at the dessert case, while my eyes darted to the over-the-top cupcake next to it. As the woman had her tongs out to grab the fritter, I stopped her. "Wait! That one. The cupcake. And, a peppermint tea. Thank you." Ford chuckled.

"And I'll take a peppermint tea as well. Thanks." He dropped a twenty-dollar bill on the counter. "Want to go find us the right table? Figure it might take you a minute to pick the best one. I'll wait for our drinks." I picked up the cupcake and nodded, but I didn't know what he meant by that. I found a table immediately—the place was practically empty other than a few random ski patrollers. But the second I sat down, I noticed the table had an unfortunate wobble. Ford wasn't looking, so I quickly moved to another table before I realized that one had a really unflattering spotlight above it. Ford might not have been here on a date with me, but I didn't need him to see the micro peach fuzz that may have been all over my face. Finally, I settled on a table between the door and a heater, which worked out great for privacy if he had his back to it. Ford sat down a moment later, smiling and handing me my tea.

"What?" I demanded, to which he broke out in a laugh.

"Nothing. I didn't say anything," he shrugged.

"So, I like to find the best table. I'm living intentionally. It all matters, you know," I said matter-of-factly.

"Where you sit matters?" he asked.

"Well, sure it does! Our time is limited. For all I know, this could be my last day on earth, and I want it to be right. It doesn't have to be perfect, but I don't want to waste it on a wobbly table that needs a few coasters squished under that third leg or lighting that makes me look like a troll living under a bridge." His eyes widened. "I mean that in a non-conceited way. Life is a gift. I want to enjoy it the best I can, is all." I took a bite of the indulgent cupcake with its double-tiered frosting. Ford laughed. "What?"

"You have a little frosting on your nose." He motioned to his own.

"I know. Maybe I'm saving that for later," I said, playing it cool before I wiped it off with a napkin from the holder on the table.

"You're different." His words dropped on the table like an anvil.

"How so?" I asked, suddenly feeling very insecure in my own skin.

"I can't quite put my finger on that," Ford trailed off.

"Is it a *bad* thing?" My words were like a whisper.

"No. Definitely not in a bad way." Hmm. I'd been told I was different before by men, all of whom didn't want another date with me. Honestly, this pattern was tiring. Was something seriously wrong with me? What if I didn't WANT to be different?

"Okay," I said back, losing my appetite for my cupcake. I only ate half of it when I set it back down on its plate.

"I'm sorry. I've been told I don't communicate very well," he admitted. I nodded.

"That's apparent," I smiled, trying to smooth things over. "And I've been told I'm overbearing. Too much. *Annoying*," I said sheepishly. Yet, saying it out loud, I felt emotion bubbling up inside of me. I had a habit of oversharing, but this made me feel small as the slideshow of hurtful comments in memory took over my brain. *Lord, I know these feelings are not coming from You. Please protect my mind from the one who is sending them.*

"I'm sorry. People can be so mean. I've experienced it, too." His words struck a chord in my heart. Was this quiet, brooding cowboy opening up to me? I wanted to do anything I could to keep it going.

"Really? Tell me about that." Okay, maybe that wasn't it. Was I writing a book? Interviewing him for a late-night talk show? Ford shrugged.

"When my ex and I broke up, half of my friends stopped communicating with me. People I'd known for years. They kind of took her 'side' so to speak, before they even knew that she left me for another man." I nodded, knowing how hurtful that must have been. "And growing up, I was treated as though I was a burden. It's not something that you can just get over that easily." I was blown away by the revelation from Ford.

"Exactly! It's more challenging to forgive people who make you feel small. Boy, do I understand that. But it's also the most freeing form of forgiveness that there is. To forgive and forget. To leave those hurts in the rear-view mirror." We sat in silence for a few minutes as Ford looked reflective, taking sips of his tea and eventually downing the rest of it. I had gulped mine down minutes ago.

"Want to get back to the slopes?"

"Sure," I said, mildly disappointed that our conversation was ending, but hoping we could pick things back up later. It took all of my strength to wobble over to the door in my stiff ski boots. You never realize how much you use your ankles to walk normally until they are frozen in place by a thick, unbendable plastic. But once said plastic is clipped into metal sticks traversing on ice, you are suddenly thankful for the lack of bendability.

We spent the rest of the afternoon shredding through the heavy, "first class" powder. Ford said it was the best snow in the world because it was a heavy, dry snow. All of that went over my head as I wasn't a meteorologist, but having grown up in Denver and skiing all around the states, I agreed that these were some supreme conditions.

Each time we got on a chair lift or inside a gondola, Ford would stiffen up. Worried that someone would be waiting in the wings at the top or would recognize him from one of the many passing chairs going by. I didn't think these fears were irrational, and he certainly didn't voice them, but rather I felt in tune with him. I picked up on things more than the average person, which was another reason why most men found me annoying to be around.

Normally, when I thought of such things—thoughts planted by the devil, perhaps—I would fall into a spiral of *dwelling.* How I was not good enough. How I had failed. How I needed to work on myself or change completely. But just then, I felt as though the mouth of the Lord was speaking into my mind: *Those you've met were not good enough for you.* I didn't deserve that treatment from them. I was barking up the wrong tree for men to begin with because they didn't deserve *me.* What a freedom it was to find peace in the Lord!

As we sat in silence on the chairlift, and God was working out my biggest hangups in life in my heart, my attention turned back to Ford. At first, I thought he was just a brooding, grumpy cowboy living in a fancy ski town. Spending time with him the last few days, I had found his demeanor starting to soften. He certainly had much more going on than met the eye. What was that phrase? *A still water that runs deep.* Just because he wasn't speaking so much that he was constantly blaring his words didn't mean he was not thinking. Or *feeling.* There was more to Ford than met the eye—but what did meet the eye was unbelievably handsome. He was drop-dead gorgeous. The winter games were just a day away, and then my trip was coming to an end. Power could have been restored to my chalet at any moment, and roads would have reopened. Would I have been able to peel back the proverbial onion of Ford before I left Sage Mountain?

CHAPTER 8: FORD

SHORT SNOWMAN, LONG STORY

The Lord sent Presley to me, because He'd been trying to reach me in other ways, and I wasn't getting the messages. That was the only explanation for how someone could speak the language of my heart so naturally.

When Presley brought up forgiveness today, it was all I could do to stay seated, as I nearly toppled over when another weight was lifted from me. One that I had been carrying for so long, the entirety of my life. I wanted to forgive those who had hurt me. *Oh, Lord, now I see that even the hurt was a gift, as every hardship is, because through our pain we find You.*

I had really enjoyed my day with Presley. She was outgoing in almost a strange way. I didn't mean that negatively; it was just foreign in today's day and age that someone be so open and honest without fear. Presley had no hidden agenda or tricks up her sleeve.

And we did share a moment; one that I had to try very hard to remember the boundaries I had asked God to instill in me. The respect I wanted to show this woman. In another life, I would have wanted to kiss her. . . Heck, in *this* life I wanted to kiss her. I still very much did. But that was something that I didn't want to cheapen. If it were to happen, I wanted everything to be out in the open and that it would be a clear, God-ordained relationship. I was done with empty relationships that had no foundation, no promise, and were full of secrets and lies.

The girl also knew her way around a ski hill, which admittedly, I found very charming. As we walked back to the chalet late afternoon, I found myself laughing hard for the first time in ages, as she recounted the splits she did when I knocked her out of the way from that snowboarder. Presley was so animated and entertaining. I found myself looking forward to seeing Priscilla, too. Still, I couldn't think of her name without smirking.

When we reached the chalet, the snow was blowing off the roof like puffs of smoke. The wind was picking up, which could have meant some major drifts tonight. As Presley went on about how much fun she had, I set the skis down outside in a snowy bump reserved for just that. She poked the poles into the mound, and we both went to the door. As Priscilla greeted us as if we'd been away for forty days, Presley took her outside to do her business, and I found myself watching and reflecting on the day and the kind of woman that Presley was.

Poppy didn't know how to ski, which was never a problem for me, of course. But her lack of willingness to try did upset me from time to time in our very short-lived romance. I tried my best to immerse myself into her hobbies and interests; why didn't she want to do that with me?

Looking back, Poppy's interests were mostly attending galas for various foundations that "big wigs" attended and shopping for those outfits. I knew this because it was my credit card coming to the rescue more than once on those shopping trips. In retrospect, Poppy likely met her now husband at one of those events. The only one I could recall us all being in the same room with was the fundraiser for the Sage Mountain Charitable Foundation. I closed my eyes and thought back to it; I thought they were raising funds to create and maintain a trail system for cross-country skiers. It was something extra for the community; a way to give back and help those who didn't use the ski mountain recreate. I personally enjoyed cross-country skiing, so I had asked Poppy if she wanted to attend with me. It was at this function that Trent Langley had been in attendance; and now that I really focused on the memories, I did recall that Poppy had been chatting with him at the champagne bar.

Poppy was fantastically good looking, in a high-maintenance sort of way. She wasn't the type of woman who could just roll out of bed, brush her teeth, and head out for the day. No, Poppy needed a team of people working on her skincare, her bronzed glow, her nails and feet, and her clothing. Poppy's hair was another story. She went to a stylist who flew in once a month from Milan. Her blonde hair and extensions didn't let her just jump into a pool or be out in the rain. Her look was curated. It wasn't a bad thing to me then, and it wasn't now, but when I compared her to Presley (whom I admitted that I did not know her beauty routine), it seemed like a stark comparison. Presley was more of a natural beauty. I'd seen her both wearing a little makeup and none—she looked great either way. Her hair was soft and in her natural color. We got snowed on during our ski day together, and it wasn't a bother to her or a big deal at all.

Poppy and Presley couldn't be more different, but the last few women I had dated were very much like Poppy: wrong for me. I couldn't put my finger on why that was, but I knew it had everything to do with God and my not waiting for the woman that He would send me.

Despite it all, I did want a woman whom I could take care of. Who would let me pay the bill at the restaurant and fill that traditional role of a wife. I didn't care if she worked, and the housework could be done by a paid cleaning service, but my dream for my life was to have a woman who was present. Not overwhelmed by the burdens that came from keeping a household, job, and children in line. I wanted a partnership—someone whom I could do all of these things with, instead of a one-way thing on either of us. *Sigh.*

Today, when Presley sat across from me with frosting on her nose, I was taken aback by her willingness to share with me about her past hurts. People had not treated her as they should have, and I found myself relating to it. But what really got me was when she told me that someone told her she was annoying. That stung for deeper reasons; growing up feeling like I wasn't always wanted or a burden to my parents, my fear every time I spoke was that I was being annoying. So, I created a pattern that I didn't allow myself to voice my feelings. Or, as Presley alluded to, "to take up space." It hurt me later in my adult relationships because without ever verbalizing who I was or what I wanted, I didn't know that I'd ever been loved for who I was, either.

Presley brought her little fluffy dog back inside as she held her in the crook of her arm. "Someone is over the snow," she said giggling. Priscilla had snow all the way up to her chest from the looks of it—her little boots and the bottom of her jacker were covered in the white stuff. They went into the mud room right off the front door where Presley kept a towel on top of the bench to wipe her down. At some point during the stay, it appeared she had also brought in a blow dryer as she was now using that to warm the dog back up. I couldn't hold back my laughter this time.

"I've never seen a dog enjoy that so much." My mind thought of dogs out a car window, but they had their mouths open and tongues out. This dog had her eyes closed, mouth closed, and if she could have purred like a cat, I imagined she would have been, as Presley was taking each one of the dogs' paws, one by one, and making sure everything was entirely dry.

"She's a spoiled Victorian child in a dog suit," Presley laughed, turning off the blow dryer. "Ready for a snack-y?" she asked Priscilla in a high-pitched voice. The dog went wild; I didn't know if it was for the incoming treat or because of the mild dampness that she felt somewhere on her fur, but she started tearing around the chalet in her bright, pink sweater.

After getting a treat, she rounded the coffee table several times before coming to me and jumping up on my legs, prompting me to pick her up. I gave in immediately.

Once in my arms, Priscilla became calm and started licking my hand. Presley politely asked about doing a load of laundry to which I quickly obliged. "There's a basket in that cupboard right there," I pointed with my free arm, but when I went to open it, she shooed me away.

"I got it, thank you. You just entertain Priscilla for me." Looking down at Priscilla, who had two bows in her hair from this morning, perfectly done still, let me know she'd been sleeping all day and was likely still full of energy. I set her on the floor and squeaked one of her toys, and she went wild again.

"Do you want to order a pizza?" I asked Presley, who had just finished loading her laundry. "After that, I gotta go take care of the horses." Her eyes lit up.

"Yes, to both," she said. "I would love a cheese pizza with extra olives and to meet your horses." I smiled.

"It's settled then," I said, reaching for the phone I kept forgetting was broken. "Can I, uh, use your phone? Mine is still out of order," I said, embarrassed.

"Of course. Let me go get it," she said, slipping out of the room and returning quickly, staring at it as she walked. "Sorry, I had a lot of notifications. Here you go." She handed it to me, looking away.

I dialed the pizza place by memory; one of the only numbers I could remember since it spelled out "P-Z-Z-A" at the end of the common prefix. After ordering Presley's choice and another one topped high with meat for me, I added on a dessert. Why not? I could have used the extra calories for the Winter Games. A feeling of dread washed over me; the Games were almost here. Was this really the end of my career? It was both a freeing and paralyzing thought to imagine this being the last competition I went through. Sure, I could have come back after a long-winded break, but I took a break every year for summer, and I still felt like that hadn't been enough. Besides, in five or even ten years after a sabbatical, would my knees allow my body to do the jumps it did now? I couldn't see that happening. These were the years that I could compete, when I was still young enough to have the cartilage and agility to do so. If I was done, I was done.

I hung up the call and found myself lingering on the thought of retirement once again. It had been captive in my mind since my father had passed away, for I was too busy competing to stop and be by his side, though I wasn't given much notice to do so, which I had realized was another thing I was hurt over. I thought of the fact that God wanted to help direct my path; no, that was not it. He wanted me to follow His path. *God, I'll be obedient to you. I feel the desire to quit skijoring. Just tell me what I need to do.*

Presley returned from the laundry room, bringing me back to the present moment. "Here's your phone. They said thirty minutes; I think we have enough time to get to the horses and back, if you're really up for it?" I asked, picking up on a change in her vibe.

"Sure, I'd love to," she said. I nodded, not reading into her demeanor, and we walked to the truck outside. I opened the door for her, And she used both the door bar and the running board to climb in.

"Sorry, I need a huge vehicle for towing trailers. But I know it's a real pain to get into with sore legs from skiing."

"You got that right. I don't think my legs have ever felt wobblier than they do right now. Totally worth it, though." She smiled and shut the door. I walked around and climbed into the driver's side, turning the ignition.

We sat in silence on the short, few minute drive to the horse stables. When we arrived, Presley cleared the air.

"On my phone, when I looked at it? There were all sorts of news stories about the Winter Games and how some competitors are cheating. Lots of allegations about riders being bribed to be throwing races and…" She trailed off, but she didn't need to say any more. I already knew it all.

"Unfortunately, there have been some bad decisions made as of late for some of my competitors. But know that I am not one of them, and you have my word I would never do that. I actually have my manager looking into proposing safeguards to prevent it from happening." She seemed satisfied with this answer, but despite dodging questions on the matter for months, I realized I wasn't done talking about it. So, I told her everything. About the allegations made against some in the sport, and that included several people I knew and had competed against, who were are now facing disqualification. The doing of which may have had me win some categories by default, which did not sit right with me.

"Thank you for sharing that with me. I'm wondering if your winning streak is what spurred this cheating scandal. They just can't seem to win against you otherwise. . ." Presley trailed off.

"I'm certainly not guaranteed to win. God has brought me this far, but I'm due any day for a humbling." My words felt foreign coming out of my mouth as I admitted that God was the reason for my current success, and, despite my joke, I feared losing. Not for how it would make me look, but rather for how it would make me feel. Was this where my deep, overwhelming pull to retire while I was still good at the sport came from? My fear of losing?

"God will get you through it. If He wants you to win, you will. And that goes for everything in life. If we get a job, if we marry. All of our days are written in His book. So, no need to fret about it, right?" Presley's words hit me right where I needed to hear them. I thanked her.

We got out of the truck and Presley ran to the stables. The air was frigid; the horses were eager for carrots. I started pulling out the bag of plump, brightly colored heirloom carrots, and they ran to me, leaving Presley in the background.

"Hey! I may not have carrots, but I have quite a bit of love to give over here," she proclaimed to the horses, who didn't look back.

"Here, take these. They will be your best friends in no time," I said, as I handed her the remainder of the bag. She giggled joyfully, and she doled them out between the group, while I shoveled in a few pitchforks' worth of hay for each horse.

"Which horse will be with you in the Winter Games?" she asked.

"Buckshot. That one, there on your right." I pointed to the towering animal.

"What a beautiful group of animals. I've always wanted to learn how to ride horses. Maybe I'll take riding lessons this summer. There's a ranch not too far from Denver that offers them."

I wanted so badly to say that I would teach her to ride. That she could take her pick from mine, throw on a saddle, and we could ride right now. But it was frigid cold, way too much snow, and I didn't know if I'd ever see her again after this week. Yet, right now, all I could think of was ways that we could make that happen. *God, I feel something brewing inside of my heart with this woman.*

"Do you want to make a snowman?" Presley asked me, and my eyes squinted together.

"Right now?" I asked in disbelief.

"Oh, come on; it's not *that* cold. Plus, we still have one carrot, so he already has his nose!" I watched in awe as Presley immediately got to work on the snowman next to the horse stable, while I had no other options but to join her.

In seconds, I was laughing harder than I had in years, possibly ever, as I watched Presley try to roll a large snowball for the body of the snowman. The snow was past her knees, and she had to lift her legs up as high as they could go just to wade through it. I joined in her effort and together, we had the first piece done in just a few minutes.

"Boy, that was quite a workout. I don't know if I have it in me to create two more giant snowballs for this guy. He might just be really short."

"You're really short, you know that?" I asked her, as I peered over at her. I was bent down, trying to secure the base for *her* snowman project when I felt a cold rush of wet hit the side of my face. She hit me with a snowball.

"Ha! How's shorty now? Pretty strong, eh?" If I hadn't been so stunned, I may not have retaliated with a snowball of my own. Soon, we were in a full-blown war. The last snowball was thrown by Presley, and it partially went into my mouth. I crunched the snow and smiled.

"Mmm. Yellow snow," I joked, as this was the fresh powder that had just fallen, and my horses hadn't yet peed anywhere near it.

"Sick!" she called out, laughing hysterically. "You're silly when you want to be," she said. I took that as a compliment.

"Okay, come finish this sad little snowman before our dinner arrives," I said. Together, we quickly packed together one larger mass of snow for his head. Presley poked two holes for his eyes and stabbed it with the carrot for his nose.

"It ain't perfect, but it will do," she said. Buckshot, knowing the sound of the crinkling bag that held his carrots, poked his head out the barn doors. He spotted the carrot and quickly came over to pluck it out with his teeth.

"And there it is," I said laughing. "It was nice knowing you, snowman. Well, we better get back for those pizzas. Unless you think Priscilla can sign for them?" Presley laughed at my joke.

"Yeah, I'm starving. That half cupcake for lunch did not go as far as I needed it to." She threw her hands up in the air to show the horses she was out of carrots.

"Better show them your pockets are empty, too, or else they will be coming for them. They know all of my tricks," I said. Presley immediately pulled out her coat pockets, showing her hands like a blackjack dealer.

"Okay, I think we're good here. We're all friends now. I had a talk with Buckshot, and he's going to be the best he can be on Saturday," she beamed.

"Is that so?" I asked.

"He seems like a very sweet soul." I wondered just how she picked up on the truth like that so quickly. They were all sweethearts, but Buckshot was in fact, my best-mannered horse out of all of them.

As Presley walked back to my truck, I put away my pitchfork and dimmed the lights for the horses, closing the barn door. Every bone in my body wanted to make sure I opened the door for her, but by the time I made it over, she was already inside. I took a beat to see the outline of a beautiful woman riding in the passenger seat of my truck, and I knew that I was ready for love—and I prayed this was the woman whom God was sending for me.

Back at the chalet, we made it just in time for the delivery to arrive. A delivery car pulled up right as we were walking inside.

"Ford?" the man called out.

"Guilty," I said, as he shuffled his pizza boxes to shake my hand. "Been a long time, Ben. How's that beautiful family of yours?" I asked. He nodded and smiled.

"They are fantastic. You know, my little man John wants to get into skijoring, just like you. Every time he sees you on the television, he's just enamored with how cool it is. When I saw your order come through, I knew I had to deliver it just so I could tell you that." A feeling caught on in my heart, followed by the realization that I would love to teach youth the sport. Was this something that was in my future?

"You tell John that he can come practice with me whenever dad says he's old enough. Of course, you can ad lib my words as needed there," I smirked. "Thanks, Ben. Hope business is doing well for you." I gave him cash and a generous tip and took the boxes in exchange.

"Business is good. The only thing that would make it better is if the town could fix this power issue. We can only run one of our pizza ovens on our generator." He shrugged but thanked me and went for his car.

"You hear any updates on that? I've been a little out of the loop," I asked.

"Nothing much, but they are hoping to get it repaired by the weekend. All will be lost if they aren't back up to full capacity at the ski resort for the folks coming in for the Winter Games." Ben turned and looked past me to see Presley's silhouette in the window. "I'm happy for you, Ford. Good luck this weekend—John and I will be cheering you on." I considered telling John that Presley was just my neighbor, and I was putting her up but instead, I relished in the good feelings of having the appearance of a relationship. John was a good friend of mine before Poppy—that relationship had been an isolating one in many ways. After our demise, I fell off the face of the earth. Seeing John made me realize I was ready to make up for lost time.

"Thanks, buddy. It was nice catching up. See you around," I called out, heading inside before the pizza got cold.

"Who is ready to eat?" I hollered out. Priscilla ran to greet me as if the food was for her. Or, perhaps she was used to getting a few table scraps at home? I smirked at the thought.

"It smells amazing," Presley said, as she quickly set the table with plates and napkins. A bottle of ranch dressing was sitting in the center, along with a container of parmesan cheese that she must have brought with her. I set the boxes down on the table and pulled up a chair.

"The owner of the place is a buddy of mine. He makes the best pizza on this side of Italy," I said.

"So, you've been to Italy?" Presley's eyes widened as she sat down across from me, taking in our conversation.

"Oh, yeah. I was invited there once to skijor. They have a pretty big following for it in Switzerland, and they had an Italian group who wanted to host it at the base of the Dolomites. I was only there for a weekend; can't say I took in any of the sights." The painful memory of my father passing away while I was there came rushing back. "But I did have a pizza, and the experience was life changing. This pizza is *almost* just as good," I laughed, wanting nothing more than to grab a slice of pizza, but I found myself waiting for Presley to pray before we ate. After a moment, she closed her eyes and clasped her hands, and I followed suit.

"Dear heavenly Father, thank You for this food we are about to eat. May Ford and I continue to learn more facts about each other, and may we draw closer to You every minute of the day. Amen."

"Amen," I croaked out. Taking a sip of the water that Presley had poured for me, I watched her pick the largest piece out of the box that was hers with a childlike awe.

"This is going to be so good," she said, as she drizzled a heaping pile of ranch dressing on her plate and sprinkled the pizza with fresh parmesan. Watching her ready the slice that I was certain she was starving for showed patience that I'd never known myself, as I was already halfway through my first slice by the time she took a bite. The pizza was fantastic, as usual, but the company made it even better. I could get used to this.

"Well?" I asked as she chewed the bite.

"You were right; this is good pizza. Not that I've ever been to Italy to compare. That's actually my dream destination."

"Really? You should go. It's supposed to be amazing in the summer," I said dryly. I had nothing real to add to this conversation since I'd only been there for 48 hours in the middle of winter.

"One day," she said, taking another bite and chewing it slowly before setting it down. "Ever since I was in my teens, I always imagined getting married there. A romantic elopement, just me and my groom, on the shores of the Amalfi coast. The sea breeze is blowing in our hair, and I'm wearing a dress I bought off the rack." As she shared her dreams with me, I felt a new connection with her. Presley was so. . . honest. Confident. *Real.* We'd spent the same amount of time with one another, and I was still struggling to open up, and here she was spilling out the deepest desires of her heart without another thought. I was beginning to feel that I knew Presley more in the last few days we'd spent together than I ever had known Poppy in our relationship that led to an engagement, that led to her leaving me.

It was then I realized that God had freed me from the shame of my past transgressions, but I was in the habit of bringing them back to light at every opportunity to do so. I needed to believe in God's forgiveness and release these hurts. To do so, I needed to forgive Poppy. I needed to forgive my parents. To forgive those who had hurt me—I could finally be free. A knock at the door made us jump.

"I'll get it," I said, standing stiffly. Who could it be? I traipsed to the door and opened it. A local delivery driver was holding a package.

"Ford Prescott? I have a package for you to sign for." He held out a handheld device for me to sign on.

"I thought the roads were still closed. How can packages be coming in?" I asked.

"This one was flown in, sir. The airport is still open. Thank you." He spun on his heels and left. The small box was marked *Overnight Air* and said it was from Jack, my manager.

"I think I have a phone again," I said, as I tore into the package. A brand-new smart phone with a heavy-duty shatterproof case was inside. A sticky note on the phone said it was already charged; I just needed to turn it on and log into my cloud account. "My manager has thought of everything. I don't think a bullet could break this casing," I mused.

I did as the note said and then I set the phone on the counter, returning to my meal with Presley. Her dog was lapping up the remains of her fancy dog food that took up more space in my refrigerator than my own.

"So, where were we?" I asked, in an effort to return to our conversation about Italy. I found myself longing for the peaceful picture she painted with her words about her dream wedding day. And deep down, I liked that she was a traditional woman who wanted marriage.

"Oh, the wedding that I'll never have," she said, shattering my previous thoughts.

"What do you mean? You don't think you'll get married?" I asked, a cautious tone to my voice.

"I don't know. I'm almost twenty-six, and I haven't had more than the fleeting first date. For some reason, I repel men! Isn't that right, Priscilla?" Presley picked her dog up and gave her a bite of the pizza crust. "But that's okay. It's all in God's plan. I trust Him; I really do. Yes, I would love nothing more than to be a wife to a godly man. However, those seem to be few and far between these days." At that moment, I felt like she was speaking directly to me. Like she could see right through me—to my past. All it took was an internet search to learn everything there was to know about me.

Presley's words struck me, and I slipped into prayer again. *Lord, I pray that Presley finds the right man for her who fulfills these desires of a godly husband. Because I don't know that could ever be me. I fall so short of that.*

In the last 24 hours, I'd prayed more than I had in the last twenty-four years. Funny how that worked. I wished I could have told Presley that her influence had started to change the man I was.

"Anyway. . . Enough of the self-pity. Do you want to watch a movie tonight? Part of my ski-trip traditions is to watch a 1980's ski flick. Unless you have an early morning. And, you are sleeping on the couch, so I don't want to be keeping you up. . ." She trailed off, talking herself out of it.

"I'd like that. And, I have just the movie in mind." I pulled out a favorite from my childhood. It was a movie that involved skiing and a mystery about a pair of missing skis and poles. The person who had them taken had to go down the ski hill on his rear end in order to get to the bottom. Very silly premise, but enjoyable and light.

During the movie, I found myself watching Presley see it for the first time. Her laughter, perfectly timed at the best parts, rang through the house. She peppered me with endless questions about the actors, about the filming location, but her passion for living in the moment was contagious. I found myself retrieving my phone so I could look up some of these answers myself, when I saw I had several missed calls from my manager.

Apparently, the phone had been powered on, but the volume had been on silent. I wished I could have gone back to ignorance of the calls and returned to the movie with Presley, but with the Winter Games being tomorrow, I really had better see what was happening.

"Excuse me for a moment—I have to call my manager."

"Want me to pause it?" Presley asked, Priscilla in her lap as she started looking around for the remote.

"No, don't bother. I've seen this so many times that I know exactly what I will miss," I said, walking into my office and closing the door so I wouldn't disturb her movie. Jack answered on the first ring.

"I hear you've been shacking up with a woman. Is that why I haven't been able to reach you?" The tone in his voice sounded very judgmental.

"You got it all wrong. It's not like that. . . But who told you that, anyway?" I asked.

"Billy. The delivery guy. I had him personally call me to tell me that the phone had been delivered. You don't even want to know what I had to pay to get that thing flown in." I groaned, knowing full well the bill would be passed on to me. The freedom of not having my phone had been so nice; I regretted that I had even signed for it now.

"Well, like I said. She's just my neighbor. Anyway, what's up? You don't usually call me this late unless something is happening," I pressed, wanting to take this conversation forward so I could get back to. . . Presley.

"Tomorrow is the Winter Games. Are you ready?" he asked, his voice still hinting at annoyance.

"Define ready," I smirked. Jack was silent. "Yeah, I'm prepared. I just have an ill feeling about this cheating scandal and what it will mean for my competition. If someone wins, I want them to win because they are the best. Not because someone threw the race," I said.

"Well, in that case, I have good news for you: The skijoring association has agreed to wipe the slate clean for those who have been suspected or accused of throwing races. But every single race is going to be monitored much, much closer with a full auditing team in place." I was relieved to hear that.

"That's great news. With these new parameters put in place, we can move on to a new generation of rules for the sport." I felt overjoyed at the defined perimeters. I was blatantly against cheating of any kind—it did not belong anywhere in sports. But now, we had formal rules against it and steps to ensure it didn't happen.

"So, is your neighbor pretty?" Jack's voice relaxed. I rolled my eyes. He'd always paid extra special attention to the ladies, as he was a lifelong bachelor who'd never been able to find the right one.

"If you must know. . . Her name is Presley. She's just. . ." I paused, trying to find the right words to describe this incredible woman, "A lot—" Jack cut me off.

"Oops. Sorry, Ford. I'm getting another call. See you tomorrow." Jack hung up.

"Okay, bye," I said to the blank phone. I didn't get to finish my sentence. I wanted to tell him that she was a lot different than anyone I'd ever met before. She was a godly woman, which was so refreshing. And she took extra care to ensure she lived intentionally in every way. As I reflected on these facts, I realized I was past the point of falling for her—I was in my feelings, deep. I considered my heart; was this a relationship from God? Saying a quick prayer about it, I realized just the fact that I was praying right now, again, was the biggest sign that it could be. This woman brought my hardened heart out of the pits of darkness, where I had been hiding from God, and back to the arms of Him.

For a moment, I thought about bursting through the office door and telling her how I felt. I wondered what she would say? Would my feelings be reciprocated? Instantly, I changed my mind; this was something that I wouldn't do lightly. I had to know, for certain, that this was the woman that God wanted me to be with before I said or did anything about it.

CHAPTER 9: PRESLEY
SKI, PRAY, MISCONSTRUE

I couldn't believe what I had heard. All of my greatest fears came true at that very moment when I decided that I would pause the movie and wait for Ford to return. I wasn't trying to listen in, but the open concept and his sky-high ceilings didn't make it hard for voices to carry in this chalet. Plus, he sounded so joyful. I wanted to hear him happy; so, I may have slowed my breathing as I craned my neck. I may have ensured Priscilla stopped chewing on her toy for a moment so I could hear the happiness exuding from this brooding cowboy. But it was then that I heard the words.

"She's just-—a lot. . ." All of my insecurities came rushing back to me. I was too much for men. I wasn't enough of whatever they thought they needed to see me as wife material. It was devastating. I quickly un-paused the movie; I would act as though nothing had happened. I wouldn't let Ford know I'd heard those words coming out of his mouth. It was too embarrassing for me to know it, let alone if he knew that I had heard it? I wanted to save myself from that confrontation.

The room felt stuffy, which was impossible, because it was quite possibly the largest living room I'd ever been in if you counted its height. I needed to remove myself from this situation—to hide from Ford. To hide from myself. *Lord, help me.*

I scooped up Priscilla and the chew bone she was so eager to continue her masterpiece on and briskly went up the stairs. I made it right before I heard Ford open his office door again. He would have seen that I was gone by now, since the office went right into the living room. My heart ached at the situation. Here I was, thinking we were jiving. The past few days were a blast. He was opening up to me and sharing. We just had an incredible day on the slopes together—and a moment I thought was worthy of a kiss. And, we had a moment where I really thought we bonded over forgiving those who have hurt us.

No matter what I recalled from the day, I felt stupid. Silly. *Insignificant.* Not only was all of that in my head—Ford did not have feelings for me like I had shamefully thought—but right now, he was probably feeling relieved to be away from me. If only I had realized this sooner! I grabbed my phone from my nightstand and looked up hotels in the area. Turned out, the books had turned. Many cancellations likely happened since the roads were still closed, and one hotel was having a special deal for tonight. I could get out of Ford's hair and let him have his bedroom back. I could leave Sage Mountain first thing tomorrow. I couldn't click the "Book Now" button fast enough. It was done; all I had to do was quickly pack my belongings, and I would be out of this grumpy cowboy's hair forever.

There was just one problem: the roads were still closed. I looked at the local community digital bulletin board for the town, and it said the tentative opening date was tomorrow. Turned out, there was a problem with the fleet of trucks they used to plow the major interstates. Some sort of manufacturer recall, and since they were all brand-spankin'-new, bought by a local donor last winter to ensure something like this would never happen, they had no other vehicles to fall back on. I went to my knees and prayed.

"God, You sure do have a sense of humor. You have my attention; there is a lesson here I am to learn in Sage Mountain, and I'm all ears to find out what that is. Just please, Lord-—spare my heart any more aching. I don't think I can handle this much rejection in one lifetime."

Once my things were packed, I tiptoed down the stairs, holding Priscilla in one arm and carrying my roller bag in the other hand, and quietly grabbed her food out of the fridge, slipping it into my bucket bag slung over my shoulder. Ford, sitting on the couch, stood.

"Is everything okay? Where are you going?" he asked. Wow. He sure did play the part of a concerned, interested man—had me totally fooled.

"A room opened up at the Snowy Owl Inn, and I'm going to get an early start tomorrow if the roads are open. I thought it best to get out of your hair," I said, playing it up that I was cool as a cucumber. After all, like a cucumber, our bodies are 90% water. Yeah, I was a cucumber that felt like I could cry at any moment.

"Oh. Are you sure you want to go there? What if the walls are paper thin? Or, what if they have bed bugs?" Why was he questioning it? He should have been relieved that he was done with me.

"What's your game here, Ford?" I set my luggage down and put my free hand on my hip while I waited for an answer. "I mean, we've spent several days together. Every meal together. Priscilla *adores* you. I thought things were heading in a totally different direction." I picked the handle of my bag back up, feeling emotion hiding closely behind my eyes, and I didn't want to give him the satisfaction. No man deserved my tears ever again. Before he could respond, I opened the door. "And then you tell your manager that I'm 'just a lot.' Well, here's a lot, Ford: I was really starting to fall for you. I mean, for who you are. Yes, you're drop dead handsome, so I'm sure you get this a lot but. . . I really was getting to know the real you. And you know what? I'm thanking you! Thank you for showing me your true colors right now, when I can still walk away. Before I'm so head over heels that I'm quitting my job and moving here to be with you." Ford's jaw dropped, and I took a deep breath. "I'm praying for you, Ford. Take care," I said, as I walked out of his chalet and his life, forever.

The tears finally escaped the corners of my eyes once I was outside. I saw him walking to the door from the window of the chalet; probably in an effort to help me with my bags. I was sure he wanted me out of there as soon as possible, after all, but it was no use. I tossed them in haphazardly, skis to follow and then Priscilla and I got in the car. I could still see my breath in front of me because it was so cold in the Yukon.

Ford was right about one thing: the Snowy Owl Inn was worn out. The walls were paper thin—thankfully, there weren't many other guests, but the guests who were there could be heard from every angle of my room. Since I hastily packed at Ford's, I was saddened to realize I had forgotten Priscilla's boots and jacket. I must have left them by the door. I was tempted to put out some newspapers for her to potty on rather than risk her catching a cold or getting frozen in the elements, but I didn't want to start any bad habits, either. So, before bed, we grudgingly took a walk down the dark and dingy hallway to find an outside area. Thankfully, she was in and out, and my blow dryer would help warm up her frozen paws.

Priscilla's Inner Monologue
This mattress is lumpy. I wish to take it up with management.

The lighting in the room was dimmer than I'd hoped, and the front desk had mentioned as much considering the town's power was still out. They had asked if I was running a lamp and a TV at the same time as a blow dryer, to unplug one item, lest they might blow a fuse. But by the looks of the place,

I didn't think that had anything to do with the power being out but everything to do with the age of the building.

Later on, when Priscilla was warm and dry and sleeping next to me in the saggy, uncomfortable bed, I longed to be back at Ford's. Swatting away those thoughts, I turned back to God, revealing my feelings and all of my heart.

When I awoke the next morning, the sky was clear for the first time since I had arrived. The constant stream of fat snowflakes had finally stopped falling. The temperature had risen by ten degrees from what it had been averaging. And after a moment, I could hear cheering from outside. I climbed out of bed; my legs were sore and stiff from all of the skiing but looking out the window and watching all of the excited skiers walk by— I wished for a moment I could join them. I opened the old window with its crank and listened to the cheers. From the sounds of it, the power had finally been restored, and the roads were reopened—right in time for the Winter Games.

I looked at my phone; my reservation at my chalet was good until tomorrow. What if I just went back there and slipped out for one last day of skiing today? Surely, the slopes would be less busy with so many attending the games. And what if, after skiing, I stopped by and was a spectator at the Winter Games?

Honestly, it would be devastating to leave this cute little town on this note, especially without seeing the event that I'd been hearing nonstop about since before I even arrived. But, did I really want to risk seeing Ford? My mind was searching for a way to bring him up and then I had it, *sigh.* As self-betraying as it sounded, I did want to see Ford. I knew that he didn't like me, and I didn't care. Every bone in my body was drawn to him and not just for his looks. I meant what I said last night—I liked him. I cared for him. And I realized it was time to pray for him, right at this very moment.

In one hour's time, the procession for the Winter Games would begin. I knew from watching it once before, many years ago, it was much shorter than the buildup to the Olympics, but also fun, with intricate takes on the sports included. There would be shots from the ice skaters, the ski racers, and the ski jumpers. Heck, Olympian Theo McCain was hosting the event—it *was* a pretty big deal. No one would blame me if I wanted to stick around and watch. I could have always taken a page out of Ford's book and worn a disguise. Ha! The idea sounded so silly and yet. . . I was racking my brain to figure out what that could be. Then it hit me: Ford didn't know I was here. The roads reopened—I told him I was leaving if they were. Surely, he had an early start this morning and was away from his chalet. I could have slipped into mine, cranked on the heat, and worn the other ski jacket that I brought in case of emergencies.

The emergency related to wearing white ski clothes of any kind almost always involved spilling hot chocolate on your coat or pants. It was always best to wear dark pants due to the risk of sitting in something, since the material of ski pants attracts stains. You sit in something once—doesn't matter if it's food, drink or grease from a chair lift dripping from the metal ropes—ski clothes cling to it, absorbing the discoloring in every level of its fibers.

That's why I always brought a second coat. Though I hadn't been skiing in years, I found this bright cherry red jacket that was more of a puffer style than my last one. I also had different goggles, which I would wear today anyway because the pair I had been wearing were for low light. These others were more of a UV blocking for brighter light. It was perfect; Ford would notice me if I was wearing my white jacket and goggles that he had seen before but now, I was in a red coat and black goggles.

It didn't occur to me immediately that it might have been strange to wear ski goggles to a spectator's event, but I didn't care. My plan was still to ski beforehand, and that's what I was going to do.

The Snowy Owl Inn checked me out in a dash, as they were pleased to get the room turned over for another unfortunate soul to experience, now that the highways had opened back up. They thanked me for staying with them and gave me a voucher for a free coffee at the shop next door, which I was grateful for since there was no coffee maker in the room.

"Oh, miss?" the front desk attendant called out to me while I was leaving, Priscilla in my arms and roller bag in the other hand. I turned back. "There's a message here for you."

Curiosity got the better of me as I wheeled my bag back to the front desk and took the note. The only problem was it wasn't legible.

"I'm sorry, someone spilled their coffee on it." The woman motioned to the man standing next to her as she rolled her eyes. The only word I could make out was "Ford." My heart sank; could he have been trying to reach me to apologize? Was there any coming back from this?

I hoofed it the few blocks to where I had parked last night; the streets were much busier this morning with people trying to pile in and out—both those who had been stranded and wanted out and those dying to get into Sage Mountain. Once I loaded the Yukon and Priscilla was securely in her car seat, I made the short few minute drive to the row of chalets.

As soon as the chalets were in view, I saw Ford's truck at the horse stables across the way. My stomach filled with nerves—both feelings of excitement and dread, simultaneously. He knew my vehicle. He would see it parked outside of the chalet. I had to think fast: Did it really matter if I was still here? Did it change anything?

After several moments of panicked reflection, I realized that it didn't matter. I didn't want to play games. He knew how I felt, and I knew how he felt. If my being here irritated him so much that he had a problem with it, that was on him.

So, I pulled into the chalet without fear. I didn't make a big deal about unloading—I just grabbed my roller bag, Priscilla out of her car seat, and calmly walked to the front door. Punching in the key codes, I held my breath; but the door chimed and most importantly, unlocked. *Thank you, Jesus, for electricity.*

Walking in, the chalet had been working hard to warm up since the power was restored. It wasn't too cold, and the heat was on full blast. I stood over the vents and felt the warmth cut through my cold hands.

Priscilla acted as though she'd returned home after being stranded on the streets. I'd never seen her so happy; she was a spoiled dog who loved luxury stays. "What am I going to do with you, Priscilla?" I asked her. She tilted her head at me and pounced. I remembered her chew toy she'd been working on carving since we got here and retrieved it out of my purse.

One last trip outside for her and I was ready to go. I looked out the window and saw that Ford's truck was gone from the horse stables. *Whew.* After last night's confrontation, I wasn't ready for another one, no matter how much I yearned to see him. And that jawline of his.

Wearing her lime green sweater, Priscilla and I made our way outside, with me coaching her to be quick about it. The weather was still warming up, so I didn't feel quite as bad about her being coatless and shoeless, but I still didn't want her getting frozen paws. The second we stepped outside, Ford was standing on my porch to greet me, holding Priscilla's shoes and jacket.

"Presley," he spoke, breathless. His truck was behind him on the road and attached to it was a horse trailer. A man was in his passenger seat; I surmised it was likely his rider.

"Hi, Ford." My voice shook as Priscilla went to him and begged him to pick her up. He hesitated for a moment, handed me her coat and shoes, and petted her on the head.

"Go potty, Priscilla," I commanded, to which she looked like she might throw a fit, but ultimately, it was freezing out, and she obeyed, walking to a clear spot in the yard.

"I just wanted to say, umm," Ford choked on his words. It was clear he wanted to make an apology of some sort, to which I accepted.

"Look, Ford—it's okay. I've been through this many times before. I'm good. I accept it, and you don't need to apologize." I put my hands up, pleading. "Go, do your skijoring. I'm praying for a win; I really am." I meant what I said. I had a feeling this man would be in my prayers for a long, long time.

"Thank you. But, last night after you left, I didn't have a way of contacting you and the Snowy Owl Inn didn't have a way to dispatch me to your room, so I left you a message, and I just wanted to ask if you would stay one more night, but seeing you here makes me think that that prayer has been answered. . ." He trailed off. So much to unpack here—for the first time in a long time, I was speechless. "There's a little starlight parade tonight after the Winter Games. Will you join me?" I wasn't prepared for any of this—here I was ten minutes ago trying to figure out a disguise so I could watch him race.

"Sure," I whispered. Normally I'd say something snarky like, "despite my better judgement." But truthfully, this had never happened before. No man had ever stood before me after getting to know me and truly wanted to see me again. That being said, the bar wasn't low—it was higher. I wanted a man just like the one that Ford was portraying at this very second, but not the one he was last night, in secret.

"Thank you. I'll meet you here—pick you up at say, six o'clock? I gotta go. We're required to show up in ten minutes or risk being disqualified." He smiled.

"What are you doing here? Don't be late! Go!" I laughed and watched as he navigated through the icy street to get to the driver's side of his truck and then drove off. Priscilla ran back inside.

"What in the world was that about, Priscilla?" I asked her, with my hand on my hip. *Lord, have I looked at this situation wrong?*

After a few moments in silent prayer, I felt a wave of energy wash over me. My sore legs aside, I was here to ski, and this was my last day to do so. Priscilla was already snoozing in her warm bed again, right where she was when we first arrived all those days ago. It was time to hit the slopes.

Skiing by myself wasn't as much of a joy as it had been with Ford. I was expecting some idle chat in the gondola like always, but today, everyone in there was foreign and speaking German. Then, at the top of the mountain, the mountain hosts were slammed with a line of people. If I were to get a consultation on my best runs today, I'd spend half the morning waiting. So, instead, I tried to remember the runs that Ford took me on instead.

All was going well until a group of snowboarders came up behind me. The snow scraping noises they made as they carved off the inches of fresh powder made me panic. Were they in control? I couldn't exactly turn around, so instead, I made an abrupt left and went into the trees. The trail in here was narrow and steeper than I thought; I was working very hard to keep my turns tight and skis tighter as I navigated through the thick wooded trail. Finally, emerging on the other side, I came up to the start of a double Black Diamond.

At first, I laughed. This wasn't going to do in any circumstance; surely, there was a way around this. But when I looked to the right and left, every part of the terrain around me formed into a lip of a bowl that this run was. The sign, indicating the run was a double black and topped with several inches of powder, read "Dilemma." It surely was that; yes.

Never in all my years of skiing had I encountered a run so daunting. I'd purposely avoided things this steep, hard, and out of reach for a reason—I wasn't ready to face them. I wasn't ready to learn the skills required of me. I wasn't ready to grow for the challenge.

I called out to God, who instantly made me think of the correlation between this run and my dating life; or at least, the pathetic attempt at one. I had let everyone who hurt my feelings over the years dim my spirit. My mind. My confidence. I was good enough to find someone who loved me for me. I was good enough to do this ski run.

"Lord, thank You for letting me rise up to the challenge. You've put the desire in my heart to find a husband, and I will not back down from it. I will also not back down from this run that I've just stumbled upon. Please keep me safe, Lord. Amen."

As I prayed out loud, I heard a familiar scraping behind me start to creep closer and closer.

Just as I was taking my last few breaths to attempt this descent at a perfect 90-degree angle, the scraping came up right behind me, scaring me as they made an abrupt stop and coating me in powder. I may or may not have screamed, scaring them in return.

The shock and fright from the snowboarder almost running into me, and the coating of powder from head to toe, freezing every part of me that had exposed skin—like my nose, mouth and wrists— sent me moving before I was entirely ready. On the steep terrain, I couldn't stop as easily as I could on a Blue or Green run; heck, even a regular Black run would have been easier than this. But this run was beyond an advanced level—this was for experts only. There was only one thing I could do in this very moment, and that was get a grip before it made its complete vertical drop. *Spoiler alert: I did not get a grip.*

I'd never screamed so much in my life. For half of the run that I remained upright and standing on my skis, my screams were coherent. For the other half where I went down on my tail end, thankfully feet first, it was more of a groan. People usually say, "It happened so fast" when things like this go down. This felt like it took forever. When I finally slowed, I wondered if I had missed the Winter Games. Was it already tomorrow morning, and I'd been gone all night? Could I just go home now?

As the sliding slowed, I reached out and grabbed a hold of an aspen tree that was next to my path. From here, I would try and regain some dignity and sense of stability. Surely, a crowd would have formed at the top of the run, and they were all holding their breath to see if I was going to slide all the way back down to base. Maybe then, I could be stopped by the security for the Winter Games. Heck, maybe I could enter the games in the "human bobsled" category.

Using all the strength I had left to get a literal grip on myself, I sat up. My skis were gone. One rogue ski pole in eyesight, but after looking at it again, I realized it wasn't mine. This must have been the skier's trail of embarrassment. There were many who came before me—those who forged this path and the things they left behind to be remembered. I made it to my feet, but my quads were trembling uncontrollably. My ears were ringing, and I felt like I had just dropped hundreds of feet in elevation in an elevator—because I had. Between the fright and the embarrassment, I thought I'd gotten my fill of skiing for the day. A quick assessment let me know nothing was broken or maybe I just had that much adrenaline pumping through my veins?

"Hey, are these yours?" a skier shouted out to me as he approached at lightning speed, holding my skis and poles.

"Nah, I think they belonged to that woman who slid down screaming. She already skied off. I'm just here hanging out." I reached for the skis as the man lingered.

"That was pretty impressive back there. This is a really difficult run; probably the hardest one I've ever encountered," he said, looking back. I followed his eyes and cringed at the fact that there was a crowd of people standing at the top and looking over.

"And here you are, having just glided down like it was a children's learning area." Clipping back into my skis, my legs felt wobbly. I could tell I was going to need a minute to get my wits about me again.

"I've practiced this run a lot. I've probably done it five hundred times," he said.

"Well, that was my first time trying a double Black Diamond. I can only say I've done a handful of Black Diamonds in my life. At least this one wasn't full of moguls. I'd probably be requiring knee surgery right now if it was," I quipped, noticing the man was about my age. Just then, he lifted his goggles up, and I saw his face. He had a boyish charm to him as he stood there. I couldn't help but notice him lingering.

"I like a woman that's fearless," he said. Wait, was he flirting with me? After that abominable scene I just put on? I was covered in chunks of ice, and my throat was raw from screaming.

"God sure does have a sense of humor," I said, to which he looked confused.

"What do you mean?" he asked, his eyes forming a squint.

"Oh, I just was up at the top of this mountain praying for my love life and protection and now, here I am, at the bottom of the run, talking to a man. It's just funny timing, is all."

"I don't believe in God," he said, the words that broke my heart to hear.

"Do you believe in the skis on your feet?" I asked. He looked down at his skis, which I noticed were a very expensive brand.

"Sure. These are from Austria. The best of the best." He crossed his arms; his ski poles going out in both directions.

"Did someone make them?" He squinted again.

"Well, of course. They are handmade by an expert artisan. Someone who spent years learning the trade and became a master at the skill," his voice softening as he spoke.

"So, if there's no God, who made all of this?" I put my arms up and marveled at the beauty of the area we were standing in. From the large mountains to the snowy aspen groves; the sky was bright and the sun was shining, creating a sparkling on every surface around us.

"There's this thing that we call 'The Big Bang'," he started to say.

"Ah. So, an explosion created everything?" He tilted his head from side to side after I asked that question.

"I mean, I wouldn't explain it like that. There's more to it."

"Like what?" It was at this point of conversation with men that they usually started to get annoyed. I had found in my experience that people do not like to question the things they have been taught or believed their whole life to be false.

"I can't explain it. I just. . . know it to be true," he said quietly.

"Sounds a lot like faith," I said. "Have you ever heard the gospel?" I asked as he looked up behind him, searching for his way out as sounds of people shredding in the snow could be heard around us.

"I'm not really into religion," he said.

"Jesus isn't a religion; it's a relationship," I said. "I don't mean for that to sound cliche, but it's true. God created the heavens and the earth and everything inside of it. He sent His one and only son, Jesus Christ, to earth, and Jesus was put to death, dying for all of our sins. When we accept Jesus into our hearts and lives and repent of our earthly ways, we are born again. Living for God means having a personal relationship with Him."

"And you have this? A relationship with Him? Or do you just think you do?" he asked. I couldn't tell if he was being snarky or genuinely interested.

"I have it. He speaks to us all the time. It's just a matter of whether you are ready to listen," I said. He shrugged.

"Well, I better go." He firmly gripped his ski poles and started to glide away.

"Will you consider what we talked about?" I asked, calling out to him. He didn't respond. *Lord, I don't know what that was—I did not have "witness someone immediately after a fall" on my agenda for the day, but I pray that seed produces fruit.*

As I started to slowly go down the terrain in front of me, I smiled. The Lord really does work in mysterious ways. Here I was, thinking He sent me someone right after that wreck. But instead, He sent me an opportunity to add another soul to eternity with Him.

"Lord, once again I am reminded that all things work together for the good of Your glory, not mine. And I thank You for that opportunity, and I pray that I can be ready if another one arises."

The double Black Diamond run turned into a Blue after I got out of the tree grove, thankfully. My tired body was ready to have some lunch and get ready to spectate the Winter Games.

Sadly, I felt that things were done with Ford and me—not that they ever had started, I meant. But I had so very much hoped that they would have been starting. Like that night we did the puzzle together—he was so sweet to join me. Or, when we had hot chocolate in the lodge. We had a spark—or so I thought. There was banter—or maybe it was his one-sided annoyance.

Ford had a past, but didn't we all? From what I knew about him from the internet and what he'd told me, he had some emotional hurdles to jump. And I prayed that when he did, and he was ready for a relationship, the right woman came along for him. I just wished that it had been me.

Once I reached the bottom, I skied until I ran out of snow and walked back to the chalet. It was time to get ready for the Winter Games.

CHAPTER 10: FORD

COWBELLS & COMEBACKS

Walking through the athlete performance tent this morning was surreal. As I looked around, I felt the excitement racing through everyone's veins, including my own. Could this have really been my last competition? Was God putting it on my heart that I was ready to move on, or was I choosing to give up? Would waiving the white flag of surrender and walking away from fame have been for myself or would it have been for God? I had so many things to consider.

Inherently, the sport was not against God. But my life these last several years had been, even when I didn't realize it. It had been against Him because it wasn't *for* Him, and that's what I was set out to change now. I didn't see that fully until now. When I decided to walk away from skijoring, it was not because I was sick of the sport. It was because my soul was yearning for something greater than I had to live for. *Thank You, God, for showing me that.*

Today, I would race as I had the last several years in the Winter Games. I would not worry about tomorrow or what was to come in my future. If I left the sport, so be it. If I stayed and competed again, it would be for God's glory.

And to think how spending a few days with a stranger—the woman whom God had placed in the chalet next door—opened my eyes to what had needed to be done all along.

"Ford Prescott." A sharp, high-pitched voice was heard behind me. Instantly, the hair on the back of my neck stood up.

"Poppy. Or should I say, *Mrs. Trent Langley,*" I said in a regretfully sarcastic tone. Truth was, I was past this. I was ready to forgive. I just needed to do it.

"You heard?" She didn't look thrilled for being a newlywed who was married to the person who ran this whole resort.

"Hard not to. It was trending between 'avalanche rescue dog team' and 'how to de-ice a mustache,' I mumbled. Ugh. How could I find the words to say what needed to be said? "Look, Poppy—" I started to hammer out a sentence, but she shook her head.

"I'm sorry, Ford. For everything. I've had a lot of time to think about my actions, and I'm not proud of how things went down with us. I want you to know that it wasn't right or fair leaving you like I did. You didn't deserve it. I'm happy with Trent, but I could have gone about those things in a much more respectful way. And I want you to know that his kids hate me. Toby is all I have left. So, the world is taking out revenge on me, ha ha." Poppy had a sadness to her as she spoke. I wasn't aware that Trent even had children. I took it all in. As much as my body wanted to hate her and tell her what I thought of saying if I ever came face to face with her, over these last few months, my heart told me otherwise.

"I forgive you, Poppy." Her eyes watered, and she started to reach for a hug but stopped herself. I wasn't about to reciprocate, not with all of these press people around. The last thing I needed was a front page in the sports section to have a large picture of me and Poppy in an embrace. The Holy Spirit felt ever present in that moment, as I remembered a verse I had heard long ago about God forgiving us and never thinking about the sins again. I wished that for myself at this stage in my life. I felt my breath releasing all of the hurt and anger, the last of which was all I had left for her.

"Thank you, Ford." Her words faded out as more and more people joined the tent. I opened up a sports drink and held it up to her, like we were going to say "cheers" to her marriage. To her new life. To my new heart in Christ. I walked away.

Reaching in my pocket, I pulled out my phone, dialing the only number I knew by heart. He answered on the second ring.

"Clint," I said, nearly falling to my knees at the sound of his voice. *Oh why, Lord, had I waited so long to forgive?*

"My brother," he said in return. "I've got the television on, and I'm waiting for your race." Tears came to my eyes. I had no idea he followed my career. I told him I'd been thinking of him for quite some time. That I'd wanted to call but felt like it was too little or too late. That I was sorry for being so distant. That I didn't drop everything to come when dad was sick. All the things that I wished I'd said to him before. He listened.

"Ford—I'm sorry for not being a present person to you when you needed it. Growing up, it was all about the farm and the livestock. I wish I could go back and make a relationship with you a priority, too. You don't owe me any apologies. I should have told you about dad sooner. This is all my fault. I pushed you away, and now I'm paying for it." That broke my heart. But immediately, I felt it starting to heal, as once again I realized I had been experiencing what conviction by the Holy Spirit is.

"How about you come out to see me next week? Or I could come to you," I offered. He laughed.

"Boy, I have never been to Sage Mountain. I've seen photos of it in a catalog, though. Do they still have that little candy store that makes the taffy?" he asked in a childlike voice.

"They sure do. Sage Mountain Sweets. And it's the best taffy you'll ever eat," I said.

"And the ice-skating rink? My wife would love that," he said. I was nearly brought to my knees when I heard he had a wife. I was so happy for him.

"There is so much to catch up on. I can send a car to pick you both up, if that's easier. You and your wife. How about Monday?"

"I'd love that, Ford. Thank you for inviting me into your life. I won't mess it up this time."

"Me either, Clint." I hung up the phone, having forgiven him truly in my heart. Now, it was time for skijoring.

"Chase," I reached out and put my arm around my horseback rider and teammate, Chase Mentock. "Are we ready to win this thing or what?" I asked, taking another swig of my sports drink while he prowled the food table, picking up a few pieces of meat and cheese.

"I'm so ready. I was up all night considering how the prize money could help us afford that down payment on the house," he said, as I noticed how puffy his eyes were.

"Yes, it's real-life changing money, that's for sure," I said, my words rambling off as I began to stress about my performance. There was a lot riding on this win, and I prayed to God right then and there that I could pull it off for the sake of Chase's family alone. My manager Jack walked up and joined the conversation.

"Well, boys. What a lovely day for a race, huh?" Jack, trying not to talk about anything that might get in our heads or cause pressure, didn't realize that I was already doing enough of that for myself.

Truthfully, I'd never considered the rider needing any of the money we won; my last rider before Chase was one of the richest people I knew and just did this for fun. The $50k he'd get in our split of winnings was chump change to him. Once, I think I even offended him when he got his portion of a smaller check. He waived it off, telling me to keep it unless it was over five grand—that I needed it worse.

Today's prize money was just over $150k. That would mean seventy-five grand for each of us. Surely, that would help put a dent on a starter home for Chase and his family. Thinking about people other than myself had consequences, as I was now worried to death I might fail somehow. I could see why I never did it before.

"Thanks for the phone, Jack," I said, holding it up. "Well, I'm going to go check on my racing skis. They were getting waxed a little earlier," I said, as I excused myself from the conversation. Jack nodded; he was too superstitious to wish us luck or so much as ask about how anyone was feeling. In his years of being an athlete manager, he said his favorite parts were securing brand deals and that watching the athletes perform gave him incredible anxiety. Suddenly, I understood that. It was because he cared about people, like I did with Chase. Like God does for me.

As soon as I was away from the group of people and standing in line at the wax station waiting for my skis, I realized the crowd of spectators could be seen from here. I scoured the crowd for a beautiful brunette with bright eyes in a white coat, but I didn't see anyone. Catching my eye was the side profile of a woman who looked very familiar in a bright red coat—one that was too bright to ignore. Kind of like Presley. She turned at that moment and smiled at me: it was Presley. I smiled back as she sat on the bleachers. No doubt she was freezing; though the Winter Games were starting soon, it was only about to get warmer for me but not for her, sitting still on a set of metal bleachers. Once I grabbed my skis and thanked the man for working on them, I gave them a quick inspection and saw all was well, then I went looking for Jack. I had a favor to ask.

"There you are," I said, finding him in the women's ice-skating competitors' tent. "How did I know I would find you here?" I cocked my eyebrow.

"I can't help it. I'm a man who loves a woman in sequins, so I'm here seeing if any of these beautiful ladies are single. Look at her—she has crystals on her eyelids." Jack looked at the women in awe. He was a nice man. I never saw him objectifying or being inappropriate around women. But he was incredibly lonely, and I wished he could find a wife. He wasn't yet fifty years old; there was still plenty of time for him to have a family, even.

"I was hoping you could do me a solid," I said, talking close to his ear so others wouldn't hear me.

"Sure. Of course, Ford. What is it?"

"There's this girl," I started out, but I could barely verbalize it. "She's magnificent," I said, drinking in the facts that I was too stubborn to see before. "And she's sitting in the grandstand right now, no doubt freezing her tail off." Jack smiled and nodded, putting his hands on my shoulders.

"I got you. Which one is she?" he asked.

"Her name is Presley. Bright red jacket, black pants. The most beautiful icy blue eyes you've ever seen."

"You know, I'm also in the market for such a woman—" I cut him off.

"Nice try. Don't go stealin' her away from me, okay?" Jack rolled his eyes and smiled.

"I'll try not to. But if she takes one look at me and decides she wants an over-the-hill, chubby, lonely son of a gun over Mr. Handsome athlete, I'm going to run away with her, but I promise to send you a postcard from our honeymoon." In our weird language, this was Jack promising me that he would go above and beyond for me. And I had no doubt he would.

Several minutes later, we were readying our places. The races were about to start. First up was Gunnar Matthias from Big Horn, Wyoming. He was a few years younger than me but had been the last few years. We'd raced in the same circles before, but I never got to know him personally. This was his first time at the Winter Games, and I was sure his nerves were over the top.

His rider, on the other hand, I'd known for years and had an infectious personality of joy.

"Mark Westerly," I said, shaking his hand. He was smiling ear to ear.

"Ford! It's been forever. Though it feels like I see you every time I open a magazine, turn on the television or walk through a sporting goods store. They got that mug of yours sprawled out on every surface!" We both laughed.

"My manager has to work long hours to convince the brands and then me; it's borderline ridiculous. I'm sorry you have to see me at all out there." We both laughed. While I was thankful for the brand deals, sometimes, it did feel overwhelming.

"Good luck today; we're up. See you next time!" Mark trotted off on his horse while Gunnar gave a salute. He was deep in concentration; that much was obvious.

"Good luck to you both!" I hollered back.

Chase and I were set to immediately follow. Any moment now, the cameras would be facing me as Theo McCain would be audible across every television and live stream in the world that was tuning in. He would say who I was and my past accomplishments. Theo would broadcast my fastest times to date and how I won the Winter Games the last few years. He might hint that it was time to pass on the torch to some younger competitors like he did when he retired from ski jumping after his big Olympic win. 25 years old isn't old by any stretch of the imagination, but in this game that requires explosive power landing jumps at high speeds, it's not uncommon to blow a knee and be done early.

The course was spread out in a giant horseshoe shape. It consisted of plastic sticks standing up together called "gates" that skiers had to go through. In addition to making it through the gates, skiers had to grab individual plastic rings that they collected on their arm by putting a hand through them like a giant bracelet. Then, there was a series of jumps, randomly placed, that the skier had to execute while remaining upright. Of course, they had to do all of these things correctly while working the 30-foot rope perfectly, and having the knowledge of what a horse might do.

The anticipation and knowledge of how a horse can and will react to certain things might be the most important part of skijoring. To be a horseman and a skier is a unique combination, and it's what's required for this sport. You also have to have the ability of not toppling over as the horse kicks up snowballs, perfectly formed by their hooves and coming at you like baseballs at a batting range. Once, I took one in the neck. It was not fun.

Thankfully, with all of the fresh snow, I wouldn't be fighting with spots of mud. Nothing ruins your race faster than a spot that's been warmed by the sun.

As I watched Gunnar and Mark go through the course, I winced when Gunnar missed going through the third gate. There was a major benefit to not going first because you could see the course with a better set of eyes, but I felt for Gunnar again as he failed to collect a plastic ring. On the last jump, Gunnar took it a little too far to the left and tried to overcompensate by tugging on the rope too hard and wiped out, having the rope pulled from him at high speed. *Disqualified.*

Next thing I knew, the cameras were all pointed to me. A television screen had my face zoomed in and you could see my cold breath in the air. As the horse got ramped up, knowing it was about to race, our time officially started when I crossed the line ahead of me. The man next to me holding my rope, so it didn't get wet, released it to me. I took a deep breath, knowing any second Chase was going to take off. I looked over to the crowd and saw Presley sitting with a fluffy lap blanket, a dozen red roses, and a hot chocolate. How in the world had Jack pulled that off so fast? I smiled and as my face was covering every sports news outlet in the world right now, including the large television that Presley was watching, I hoped she knew that smile was for her.

I had seconds left to get my head in the game. "God, please help me win. For your glory." The announcer said it was our turn and Chase and Buckshot were out of the gates with more intention and speed than I knew possible. I expertly tore through the gates, grabbing the rings like my life depended on it, and like Chase's future in Sage Mountain, a place he wanted to call home, depended on it. Because it did. The first jump, I landed perfectly; the torches lit as I rode through a checkpoint while the crowd excitedly rang cowbells in the distance. I grabbed another ring, went through several gates. The second jump, a breeze. I thought of everything and nothing at the same time. I was both holding my breath and breathing harder than I ever had in my life as the horse kicked up ice chunks that were pelting me. This race-—with Presley and my brother tuning in to watch; with people that I loved and cared about wanting me to win—I wanted to make it happen more than anything. As we turned and did the last set of gates, I heard Theo McCain say, "and this performance right here is what we've grown to expect from Ford Prescott." His words got in my head for a moment, and I nearly missed the last gate. I nearly tumbled. I nearly wiped out. But I yelled out to God at that very second and felt a renewed strength in my grip on the rope. A stronger will to remain upright. This win wasn't for me. It was for everyone whom I loved.

The last jump came and I landed it. But I landed too hard. No one knew the difference, but when my skis touched down on that snowy landscape, I felt something happen in my right knee. A slippery spot, and I overcompensated. Still, I didn't let it hold me back. My body could break, but I was going to keep fighting for those whom I cared about.

When we finished the race, I had sweat dripping down inside of my goggles. My gloves were about to slip off from the sweat inside them. It may have been just a few minutes of a course, but I felt like years had been shaved off my life. But when I looked at Chase, I knew we had just done something huge. He smiled, dismounting from Buckshot and gave me a hug; the rings around my arm were the reminder of what was just accomplished. I stood there, feeling my knee as it throbbed.

"They said it was the fastest time in skijoring history!" Jack came to me on the sidelines and kissed me on my sweaty cheek. "You've just made me the happiest manager in the world, kiddo!" Chase was already calling his wife. There were still a handful of competitors, so I wasn't sure why everyone was already thinking this was a win. I voiced that very concern.

"Sure, Ford. Someone could still win. They would just have to beat the current world record for this length of course that you just set." Jack shook my shoulders. "You are a hero, Ford. You've done something huge here. Once the shock wears off, you'll get it." Jack went on to talk to Chase.

Theo McCain's assistant came over and asked if I would do an interview after the Games were wrapped. I thought about it for a moment, having shied away from the press for several months, but changed my mind. Suddenly, everything was clear to me.

"Yes. I'd love to." She excitedly agreed and told me where to meet him after.

The rest of the competitors came and went while I took respite at the medical tent. From their analysis, my knee had no swelling and full range movement. It was possible I just landed on it too hard, and I was lucky I didn't tumble from it. At some point, Theo McCain made a statement prepared by the Wyoming Cowboy Skijoring Association regarding the cheating scandal and the measures that were in place now to ensure that it wouldn't happen. He went on to say that all accusations aside, they had no way to retrospectively prove something, but today everyone, could be assured there was no cheating involved. I was pleased with the task force on hand, and also that we could forgive and forget. It was kind of my new thing.

The rest of the competitors went, with the last one being the strongest contender. I was actually starting to feel a little worried after he took off out of the gate with his speed. He was smaller than me, which a lot of times, the lighter you are, the better, and his horseback rider was very intuitive, like Chase was for me. The skier took each jump and ring, and Chase and I watched in silence as they finished the course. My time was one minute fifteen seconds. This rider was one minute twenty seconds. I let out my breath I'd been holding in the entire time. *Lord, thank You.*

"I can't believe it!" Chase yelled. "I'm going to be okay. I'm buying a house, Ford! My family is going to own a home in

Sage Mountain." Chase had tears in his eyes. "Thank you for giving me the opportunity to make this dream come true. And for winning me $75,000 !" He hugged me.

"Chase, you did just as much as I did for that. You're an excellent rider. And about the money—why don't you take this check for yourself? Take the burden off of that mortgage a little." Chase started bawling and hugged me again.

"I can't do that, Ford. But you are such a great guy," he said weeping.

"Yes, you can, Chase. And you will. I mean it. I'll sign the whole thing over to you. I want you to be here in Sage Mountain where your family belongs," I said, and he nodded. I was blessed. I didn't need the money. My brand deals alone were what paid my bills. I bought a swatch of land here a few years ago before things really blew up, and then I had the chalets built on them. The rental income would be more than enough for me.

"I'll never be able to repay you, Ford." Chase looked at me with more joy than I'd ever seen in another person's eyes.

"You don't have to. It's my gift. Anyway, we better go," I said, looking to the grandstands. I told Presley to meet me at the chalet around six, but I had this interview to do. I would ask Jack to pass the message along but suddenly, he was nowhere to be found. I wished I had gotten Presley's phone number; I only had several days to do it. "I signed us up for an interview afterwards." Chase shook his head.

"They don't want me, Ford. They want *you.* Thank you for including me, but I have a house to buy." Chase smiled and left.

"Theo McCain," I said, walking up to the interview tent. He was all set up with a chair waiting for me.

"Ford Prescott, part of the winning team for skijoring at the Winter Games. . . How many years in a row, now?"

"I've been blessed, though I don't deserve it," I said. Theo's eyes squinted. That wasn't exactly the victory speech that a guy with a pretty big ego himself was waiting for. I took a seat, ready to bare it all.

CHAPTER 11: PRESLEY

HOT COCOA & HOT TAKES

Jack, Ford's manager, was sweet enough to bring me a warm blanket. And a hot chocolate from the athlete tent. And a dozen roses that were for sale at the florist that he walked past to buy said blanket at the luxury home store. I was completely blown away.

"These are technically from me, but Ford asked that I take care of you," he winked. He was a charming man with kindness in his eyes. "But don't go fallin' in love with me, honey. Ford said you are his." My cheeks reddened at his words.

"*Ford said that?*" It was everything I could do to keep my composure. Jack tilted his head back and forth.

"In a roundabout way, yes," he smiled, revealing his gap-tooth grin. I was blown away by his statement.

"But I heard him on the phone. Actually, he was talking to you!" I stood, needing to work this situation out in my head.

"He told you I was just 'a lot'. . . And that's it. I didn't hear anything else." My use of air quotes while wearing mittens was wildly ineffective. Jack shook his head.

"I don't really remember that, but what I do remember is he just said a few minutes ago that he wanted me to take care of you out here. And he made it clear I wasn't to go make you fallin' in love with me instead. I'd say he likes you, sweetheart." Jack smiled one last time and walked away. I was holding everything in my arms and carefully sat my drink down to handle the rest. I decided to wait until Ford raced before I would start overanalyzing the rest of the situation so I could focus all of my energy on praying for his victory.

*****

Watching Ford expertly traverse the skijoring track was inspiring; now, I knew what the big deal about it all was for. Aside from his incredible looks, he was truly the most talented skier that took the track. Once I started watching, I became fully immersed in the sport and had let everything else go.

Ford was by far the fastest racer until the last pair went. That team was almost just as fast, but not nearly as skilled in the game. Still, it seemed like the other racers didn't even compare to Ford's team in ability. I was feeling very proud by the end of it.

Since I was meeting Ford in a short while back at the chalet, I decided to go back to mine to change my clothes and warm up. Feed Priscilla and eat a good meal myself. I was very much craving something warm, cheesy, and carb-filled, but with this blanket and roses—the hot chocolate fully consumed—I couldn't really carry a pizza back with me, too.

As I started my walk back to my rental, the TV screen flashed a notification that Ford would be interviewed in the next few minutes by Theo McCain. I stood still; not sure if I had time to make it back to tune in on the television, or if I should just stay. Ultimately, I waited. I was already standing outside of the grandstands, so I wrapped the faux fur blanket around my body and bore my eyes up at the screen.

It showed Theo McCain ready to interview as another commentator spoke about racing facts and highlighted a few clips from the best moments of today's skijoring event. Then, it was cut as Ford appeared on the edge of the screen. He said a few words which were a bit mumbled, and a woman came on and clipped a mic to his coat. He had his helmet on still, but his goggles were up. He looked tired, like he was up all night. I found myself wondering how things went after I stormed out last night. Clearly, for us to go from there to him sending me a blanket and Jack improvising with flowers, something happened.

Ford took a seat, and the conversation went back to Theo.

"So, Ford, you were saying that you had something to say?" Theo looked uncertain. He seemed the type that liked to remain in control, but Ford was an athlete *and* a Wyoming heart throb, so he gave Ford the reins.

"Yes, I do. I was saying that I don't deserve to win." An audible gasp was heard around me. I wasn't the only one hanging by a thread.

"Woah, Ford. Does this have something to do with the cheating scandal? Are you admitting to the use of. . . bribery?" Theo frantically looked around to make sure the camera was rolling, and he gave someone a thumbs up. Ford shook his head.

"No. Never. I've never needed to use those tactics to win." Theo almost looked disappointed that he wasn't getting a live confessional. "And we have taken the steps to ensure there are drug tests before races, from now on. So, that 'scandal' is over." People clapped. All of that worrying and stress over the last few months was just cleared up. "What I'm saying is, I have fallen so far from God and yet, I won anyway. Today's win was all for His glory. All of my career was all for His glory!" People started clapping again, and Ford kept his eyes on Theo.

"What do you mean, 'was'?" Theo quizzed him.

"Good catch. That's the second point I'd like to make—something I've been considering a long time now. I've finally realized now is the time. I'm announcing my immediate retirement from professional skijoring competitions." Another gasp in the crowd. My jaw dropped. This handsome cowboy, the face of the sport, was leaving?

"Well, that certainly is a surprise, Ford. What's next for you?" Theo looked like all of his hopes for this interview had just been washed down the drain.

"I'd like to start a skijoring training camp and fellowship for youth. I want to give back to my community and focus on my personal life and my walk with God." If my jaw wasn't already hanging on the pavement, it was now.

"That all sounds very good, Ford. But may I ask, what brought this all on?" Theo was scratching his head with questions. I was, too.

"Of course. This week, I met someone —a woman." A few whistles were heard from the crowd. I held my breath. "And she is just a lot. . ." He paused, and I waited for a public humiliation. "A lot *different* from anyone I've ever met." Ford turned to the camera, and I felt like he was looking right at me. "She's a godly woman with morals and standards, and she does not take a moment for granted. Presley, you inspired me to reconnect to God after I had fallen so far away from Him. And I want you to keep inspiring me if you'll agree to be my girlfriend." All the color drained from my face. I had it so wrong.

When I stormed out of Ford's chalet, he didn't correct me. How was I to know what he meant—what he was going to say if he finished that sentence? My fears and past hurts had become a part of who I was. While I had forgiven the men who told me such hurtful things, I had not been able to forget. and that was the lesson I needed to learn through all of this, just as God forgets my sins after forgiving me.

Ford and Theo wrapped up their interview with a cordial goodbye initiated by Ford as he stood up and shook Theo's hand. Theo remained sitting, surely still processing what had happened.

I walked back to the chalet. My snow boots proved to be a little tricky on the icy street as I crossed it. My stomach, which was growling just a few minutes before, was now jumping. What was this feeling I was experiencing? My nerves were electrified. I thought of all the things I wanted to say to Ford, including an apology. My body felt a rush of adrenaline. This was excitement in its purest, richest form, and I wanted to savor it.

Back at the chalet, I couldn't wait to tell Priscilla everything. I originally wanted to cook up some macaroni but now, I craved something light. My appetite was almost gone, but I knew I needed to eat if I wanted energy to walk around with Ford tonight. The only food I left behind in the chalet was a small TV dinner. Perfect.

After I ate, I fed Priscilla and played with her. In this climate, I was thankful the dress code would be what I was already wearing, and I didn't have to worry about clothing. My hair was another story. I took a mental inventory of what hat or earmuffs I could wear tonight while Priscilla squeaked her toy as loud as she could.

Finally, it was ten til. Ford would be meeting me at any moment. As I brushed my teeth, my heart skipped a beat when I thought about the fact that he had asked me to be his girlfriend. I just needed to accept. Little thoughts started penetrating my mind like "maybe he's changed his mind" or "what if he doesn't show up." I knew these thoughts weren't from God, so it made it easy to narrow down where they did come from.

Years ago, someone told me that God is love. He doesn't send us doubting thoughts that make us writhe with anxiety or despair. And that we must keep our minds and hearts guarded, because the devil wants to wriggle into our thoughts and make us feel weak. Defeated. Playing our shame on repeat. This was exactly what I'd been allowing to happen in my mind for years.

"God, please give me strength to overcome these thoughts that are making me feel small. By Your grace, I have been forgiven. And help me remember that and not entertain anything otherwise for even a second. I don't want to waste any more time on my past." Praying felt so good that I forgot I was still holding a toothbrush when a knock came to the door.

Priscilla started barking her head off, alerting me that someone was there. "Come in," I called, since I knew it was Ford, and heck, he owned the place.

"Presley?" Ford called out.

"I'll be right down," I said, quickly spitting out my toothpaste and doing a mouth rinse. Sparkling clean.

"How is my favorite little dog doing?" Ford said, loud enough for me to hear as I was coming down the stairs, dressed in my ski clothes from earlier but wearing a black wooly hat with a fuzzy ball on top. And with makeup on. Waterproof, because nothing makes your eyes water more than the cold air.

Priscilla's Inner Monologue

What, no flowers for me? Don't tell me Jack couldn't send a charcuterie tray. Amateur move, Prescott.

"Hi," I said, my voice shaking. "I just want to say something," I said. I couldn't stop trembling. I took a few steps towards him, but Priscilla was running laps around us and we both laughed, lightening the mood.

"No, you don't have to say anything." Ford shook his head, but I put my hand up.

"Please," I held my hand in the air. "I'm sorry. I made a horrible assumption based on my own baggage. I just want to let you know that I have let all of that go. And, if the offer is still on the table..." I crossed my arms gently, trying to tiptoe around the relationship question because I couldn't let it go. I wanted to lock this in.

"Presley—let me do this right," Ford asked, smiling. "I also would like to apologize for holding back. I had some forgiving to do, too. It's done. I am free from the burden of hurt. And yes. I would like to date you. Or, rather, court you. I want to do this right. Once a boundary is crossed, you can't put a genie back in the bottle. You know what I mean?" I smiled, knowing exactly what he meant.

"No more living together. Check," I put my hands up in reference to being in my own chalet.

"Exactly. It's just that things can happen. And I know firsthand how easily temptation can take over. But I've been forgiven of my past. If that's not a dealbreaker for you that I have a past. . ." he trailed off.

"No, it's not. The only dealbreaker would be if you didn't see that as wrong because I am abstaining from those temptations . . .until marriage, I mean," I said. "Not that I would be opposed to a kiss, but you are right. Things get out of hand, and I don't want to lead with lust. Yes, I am obscenely attracted to your looks. But if we are going to do this, I want to focus on what's inside." My cheeks were reddening. Not because I was ashamed, but rather, it was awkward talking about something related to physical affection. Ford smiled, and it quite possibly was the biggest smile I'd ever seen on someone.

"I love that about you. And I respect that and want the same for my life. To save myself, who was once tarnished but has since been washed clean in the Holy Spirit, for my future wife." I clapped my hands together in joy.

"It's so nice agreeing on physical boundaries at the start of a relationship," I said.

"Does that mean you want to date me? To agree to this courtship?" He looked at me with a smirk.

"Yes. On one condition," I said, letting him sweat for a minute.

"Okay, sure. What is it?"

"You get a generator in this chalet, because I have a season pass for skiing and a cute cowboy boyfriend in the chalet next door." Ford playfully pulled out his phone and dialed a number.

"Hello? Property maintenance team? This is Ford Prescott, and I need an emergency generator delivery and hookup." I laughed and thanked God for all of the blessings He had given me and the lessons He taught me along the way, while I waited for a kiss from my new boyfriend.

EPILOGUE: PRISCILLA

PRISCILLA APPROVES OF THIS MESSAGE
NEXT WINTER

I wish someone would tell my mom she can't carry a tune. If only I could talk, I would break the news to her. But right now, I don't even care that she's belting out *Elvis* at the top of her lungs because the long car ride can only mean one thing: We're visiting my favorite person, Ford.

"Priscilla, do you think that Ford has anything fun planned for us this week?" Mom always asks me rhetorical questions. We both knew the ring was coming; it was just a matter of time. We've been coming out here so frequently that I don't see why we don't just live here by now. I'd surely enjoy living in that nice, cozy chalet. Especially now that the chimney has been fixed and my mom can start as many fires as she wants. . . with Ford's help, of course.

Ford came out to see us last month. Well, he says he's visiting my mom, but Ford and I both know that he can't get enough of me, either. Which is good, because Mom and I are a package deal. He stayed at a fancy hotel, which was very much to my liking—it smelled like *Chanel* perfume and had art that rivaled a museum, because they took me with them to one of those, too. I get to accompany all of their dates after that misunderstanding that me and my mom had.

Honestly, I knew what I was doing. I couldn't bear the thought of being left at home while Mom and Ford were out gallivanting without me. So, I might have "acted out," as Mom calls it whenever I do something she doesn't approve of. All I did was replace my chew bone for one of her purse straps. It was one I haven't seen her carry in a while—and frankly, by the style and color, which was *so* last season. I was doing her a favor. That purse was never going to help progress her relationship with Ford.

When she got home and discovered my assistance in her fashion choices, she ordered a deluxe stroller that looked like something a nanny for a billionaire might be pushing around. It had gold wheels and a cozy, black carriage. Very much up to my standards, I approved of it immediately. Mom says God made me too cute for my own good. And now, I get to tag along everywhere. I don't miss a thing. Problem solved.

One day on Ford's most recent trip to see *us,* he took us to lunch. I was pleased that he ordered the steak—we both like ours cooked to medium rare temp, so he shared with me. Afterward, we went for a stroll in the park. It was getting very cold out, and I started to shiver since he hadn't noticed me in a few minutes. He immediately remedied the situation by taking me out of the stroller and suggested we go inside some shops. I wished I could tell him my favorite couture brand is just down the street—*Robbins & Barks.* They have the nicest sweaters and hair bows.

Mom was excited to go into some stores; I could tell she wanted to stop by my store, too, but suddenly, Ford suggested we go to the jewelers. Fine, I thought my collar could use some rhinestones. Then, Mom got all quiet and weird, which is only half like her. He walked over to the ring case and asked Mom which one she liked the best.

I gotta hand it to her; despite some questionable purse choices, the woman can pick out a ring that makes me proud. After quite a bit of awkward fumbling, she tried a few rings on and said that the emerald cut solitaire was her favorite. I was so relieved that she didn't say princess cut; after all, that is my signature diamond.

When we got home that night, Mom called everyone she knew to tell them that she'd just got home from ring shopping. Half of them sounded a little *too* surprised, which I took as a personal insult. Here I am, working my tail off to help charm this man so that he marries my mom and I can nap on that cozy couch of his in Wyoming forever. And they doubt my charm?

"We're almost there, sweetie," Mom says, popping my daydream bubble. I feel the excitement washing over me as I sense Ford is near; I can almost smell the hints of hay on him. My tail is wagging faster and faster as we pull into the driveway of the chalet next door to his. I look up and see him! Ford is walking over to the door to greet us!

After he greets my mom with a *kiss,* I let out a whine. Where's my kiss on the head? Finally, he comes over to my side of the vehicle and plucks me out of my car seat. Reunited at last.

When we walk into the chalet, Mom makes a big deal that it's decorated to the nines for Christmas. It appears that Ford has put up a freshly cut fir tree, and it's covered in beautiful lights. After some detective work, I find the tree has a wonderful water bowl for me below it. There are also a few presents scattered about—if he has the sense that I think he does, many of these will be for me.

"Merry Christmas, Priscilla," Ford says as he hands me a present and says I can open it whenever I please. I stick my head in the bag and smell a high thread count outfit. I'm pleased.

That night, as he is in *our* chalet for dinner—as in the same one he always puts us up in—he says he has a surprise for Mom. I look up, noticing I am not included. *Is there anything I can chew in the general vicinity?* Mom asks him what it is, but he says she has to wait.

Later, Mom runs upstairs to get ready. We are going on a winter stroll tonight. Mom got me a heated bed for the stroller so I will stay cozy, but I'd prefer to just be in Ford's jacket. Keeping him wrapped around my paw, where he belongs.

"I have a secret," he whispers in my ear. I look up at him and wag. Yes? What is it? I wish I could speak. Instead, I let out a small bark.

"Tonight is the night. I'm proposing at the gazebo. It's covered in those little twinkle lights, and a woman with a harp is going to risk the cold air to play a little song. What do you think?" *Yeehaw!* I think. I've successfully charmed this man into marrying my mom! But he doesn't stop there. "I'm thinking of giving her these plane tickets, too. What do you think?" He pulled out an envelope that contained some paper that I'm assuming are tickets. I don't know. I may be a pampered pooch, but I still can't read. He read my mind. "Two first-class tickets to Italy. And you get to come, too. If she says yes, that is," he laughs under his breath. If only he knew how much Mom was praying for this day to happen. Then again, I think he does.

When Mom comes walking down the stairs, she looks like she is walking out of a ski catalog. She has the snow pants that look like leggings—I cringe to remember they have stirrups at the bottom. If only I could give her some advice: *Please Mom, do not remove your shoes in his presence.* A white turtleneck makes her complexion even more glowing. Soft makeup on her cheeks and a fuzzy hat. She really does look beautiful. I love my mom.

"Wow," Ford says, agreeing with me. "You look amazing." He stands, taking me with him.

"Thank you," she says, walking towards us. They kiss *again,* which I am ready to get on with the night. Thankfully, she is thinking the same thing. "Are we ready to go?" Ford nods, placing me in the stroller. Um, are you forgetting something, darling?

"Priscilla just needs her coat," my mom says, realizing the problem immediately. Ford nods, quick to rectify the situation, and puts me in my winter coat. And off we go, me in my luxury carriage that glides through the snowy landscape, Mom and my future dad, with his arm linked in hers, as we venture off to the gazebo to start our future as a family.

"We love because he first loved us," 1 John 4:19. And under the twinkling lights of Sage Mountain with a fresh blanket of sparkling snow, love had only just begun.

ABOUT THE AUTHOR

Cassandra discovered her passion for writing at the age of seven when she purchased a diary at the Scholastic Book Fair. What began with journal entries about her school and home life later evolved into a collection of poems, short stories, and novels. Her hobbies include skiing, traveling around the Rocky

Mountains, and reading. Much of her writing inspiration stems from her love of dogs, her Onondaga heritage, and her Christian faith. Cassandra's favorite genres of books are Christian fiction novels, Thrillers, and anything British.

She is a full-time writer and resides in the mountains of Wyoming with her husband, Chad.

Find her online at cassandrajoelle.com

OTHER BOOKS BY CASSANDRA

How to Fall for a Cowboy: An All-Pumpkin, No-Spice Christian Romcom

She's Glossy Nails. He's Flakey Crust. The Plan? Half-Baked.

In the town of Maple Haven, Wyoming, Autumn isn't just a season- it's a celebration. Ginger Hart is spending the season like she has for the past year: hopelessly crushing on Dallas, the gym bro who communicates in motivational quotes. In her quest for his attention, Ginger's lost more than a few pounds- maybe, a bit of herself. As the town gears up for the annual Pumpkin Stampede, something (or rather someone) rolls into town in a pumpkin-themed dessert truck parked right outside Ginger's salon. Behind the counter? Ex bull-rider Tucker Callahan. He's all cowboy hat and delicious sweets- basically everything Ginger's been trying to resist. When they decide to fake date for his image and for her to get Dallas' attention, he proposes one sugary-sweet condition. As cozy sparks fly, Ginger begins to wonder if God's sweetest plans aren't always the ones we bake up ourselves.

Genre: Christian Romantic Comedy

A Weather Girl's Guide to Love: A Thunderously Sweet Christian Romcom

Partly Cloudy, Mostly Complicated.

Hailey Sinclair had her life all mapped out- until God changed the forecast. Instead of being an on-air meteorologist for a national network, she's reporting the weather in rural Wyoming. Now she's caught between her college sweetheart, Jett Dawson, and Colt Wilder- the infuriatingly gorgeous and cheerful cameraman who seems determined to break through her stormy exterior. Torn between the future she planned, and the one God might be writing, Hailey must learn to trust His direction- and her heart- even when it leads straight into the eye of the storm.

Genre: Christian Romantic Comedy

A New Leash on Life: A Dog-Mom Rom-Com, Book 1

Get ready for a hilarious Christian romantic comedy as we follow the journey of a thirty-something introverted woman, Katie Fitzgerald, who's longing for a husband. But when she accidentally adopts a dog, she discovers that love comes in unexpected ways, and that God's timing is always perfect.

Genre: Christian Romantic Comedy

Fetching Love: A Dog-Mom Rom-Com, Book 2

Three couples, three journeys, and one hilarious adventure on the unpredictable path to love. Katie and Eli are ready to say "I do," but the days leading up to the wedding are full of surprises- especially when Katie's mom's true crime sleuthing lands her in a pickle. Samantha and Mitchell seem perfect together, but hidden struggles test their relationship. Can they find common ground, or will their opposing desires pull them apart? Carolyn and Micah have found faith and each other, but their surprise romance leads to a sudden, life- altering decision. As these couples follow the Lord, they find joy and laughter along the way.

Genre: Christian Romantic Comedy

The Après-Ski Proposal: A Romcom About Love Off-Piste

She came for a fresh start... Not a fake boyfriend. When Claire Riley gets dumped on the eve of her 30th birthday, she's blindsided. A spur-of-the-moment ski trip seems like the perfect escape, until she runs into her ex... With his new girlfriend. Shocked and desperate for a lifeline, Claire accepts a proposal from a charming stranger to pose as her fake- boyfriend. What begins as a simple act of saving face turns into a journey that reveals a fresh start in life and love—the kind that only God could have planned.

Genre: Christian Romantic Comedy

The Curse of Josephine Bagley

Over the course of a century, three individuals are woven together by a decades-old curse:

William, after surviving an Indian raid on his orphanage due to his facial disfigurement, goes on to live among the tribe.

But when misfortune befalls them, he is quickly traded away and faced with a pivotal choice that changes his life forever.

Josephine has faced immense loss. Despite her granddaughter's efforts to help her find solace in faith, she finds she can't let go of the past and falls further into her belief that she's eternally bound to darkness.

Saraphina, a fledgling antiques dealer, gets the surprise of her life when a courier delivers notice that she's the last surviving relative of the Bagley Estate. What seemed like a windfall that could help her career now causes her to question her own reality.

In this tale of intertwining mystery, loss, and faith, these souls navigate through nefarious trials to find the gift of grace and forgiveness that extends to us all.

Genre: Christian Gothic

www.ingramcontent.com/pod-product-compliance
Lightning Source LLC
Chambersburg PA
CBHW032241310726
48973CB00008B/2245